Mari Stead Jones was born in Preston and still lives in the north west of England. This is her first novel.

Stead Jones, born Thomas Evan Jones in 1922, was brought up in Pwllheli, north Wales. His first novel *Make Room for the Jester* was published in 1964 in both the UK and the USA to much critical acclaim. *The Ballad of Oliver Powell* followed in 1966, and then *The Lost Boy* in 1968. He carried on writing until he died in 1985.

Say Goodbye to the Boys

Mari Stead Jones

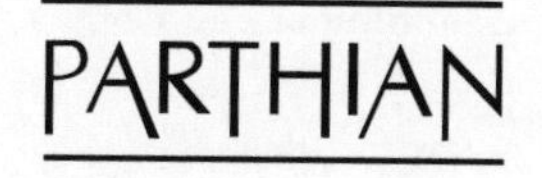

Parthian
The Old Surgery
Napier Street
Cardigan
SA43 1ED
www.parthianbooks.com

First published in 2013

ISBN 978-1-908069-97-9

The publisher acknowledges the financial support
of the Welsh Books Council.

Edited by Jon Gower

Cover design and typesetting by Claire Houguez

Printed and bound by Gwasg Gomer, Llandysul, Wales

British Library Cataloguing in Publication Data

A cataloguing record for this book is available from the British Library.

For my father and my daughter

I

It was a good place to be, even with Laura standing at the foot of the bed delivering the Sunday morning sermon. It was the best of all possible places – father's house, 21 Liverpool Street, Maelgwyn-on-Sea, my old room above the kitchen at the back of the house, a church bell ringing in the town, and a blackbird in good voice in the yard outside. Even with a head full of beer and fags, a good place to be.

'Don't pretend you're asleep! What about your shoes for a start?' I stiffened under the sheets. I had socks on my feet. 'What time did you crawl in this morning, I'd like to know? Smells like some old brewery in here. And you were such a refined little boy.' She prodded me. 'Too ill to talk are we? Whatever were you thinking of – leaving your shoes there for all the world to see?'

My shoes! My demob shoes! Oh good God, I'd taken them off at the front door, hadn't I? Carried them upstairs hadn't I?

'Full of water, both of them! At least I think it's water. But what did the milkman think? And all the people on their way to chapel; what did they think? Don't tell me no lies boy! It was past three when you came in because it didn't start raining till half past. Not one wink of sleep have I had. Not one tiny wink. You left them in the rain, didn't you?' A long despairing sigh. She had moved to the window now, her voice husky with complaint. 'You know how I've been – ever since that old war started, not been able to sleep a night through.'

Quite mindless, had been my father's judgement on her – Laura Roberts, his second wife, my stepmother – quite mindless, but very kind. Now she was back at the side of the bed. 'And you were such a good little boy, Philip. Talk to me.' Silence she couldn't bear. 'Wherever were you till that time? Why did you leave your shoes there for all the world to see?' For Laura all the world was Liverpool Street. 'You and those friends of yours...'

I sat up and pulled the sheet clear of my head.

'Oh,' she cried out, 'look at your eyes! Debauchery, that's what you've got! How long is this going on for, Philip?'

Forever, I hoped. Forever and ever! Back home in the one good place, soldier from the wars returned. But that was before the days of madness and death.

Maelgwyn town was still and quiet and full of dusty sunlight that Sunday morning, echoes of hymns in the air. Liverpool Street was in the old town, near the Market Hall where my father had his shop. A neat, terraced street, not poor, not rich, with doorsteps making black, polished statements all the way along. My shoes, brimming with water, must have sent the chapel-going brows flapping. Once down the High Street the town changed, bricks and pebbledash and stucco replacing stone, and houses growing larger, taller, with rooms abounding, all the way to the sea front, and the Promenade. Yet it was here, in the newest, grandest part of town, that shabbiness showed.

Peeling paint and flaking plaster, windows without curtains and empty houses, scars of war everywhere in spite of the fact that not a shot had been fired at it, not a bomb dropped. Here no visitors had arrived for six long summers. And here there had been a kind of occupation – by Civil Servants, by the Royal Air Force, by the Yanks. And the bruises showed.

'Some of them were animals,' Laura had told me. 'Not all of them, mind. Burton was a very nice boy. Been to college and everything.' Burton had been a Lieutenant in the US Air Force. Burton had married my sister Gwen and taken her back to Baltimore. And anyone who had taken Gwen on must have been all right. Must have been a bloody saint too!

The wind was coming in off the sea. There were big ships out there whose dialogue of sirens you could hear, especially at night, all of them waiting for a tide to take them the last six miles up to the port. Maelgwyn-on-Sea the town wanted to be called, but it was on an estuary, and its beach was pebble and estuary mud, and dredging was a dirty word. You retired to Maelgwyn, and there were elderly men with elderly dogs at the water's edge to prove it. But now the barbed wire had gone. Only one concrete pillar box remained from the war, and there was talk of converting that into a public toilet. It seemed fitting.

Emlyn Morton waved from the deck of the *Ariadne* in response to my whistle. Yachts and fishermen's boats were strung in a line along a muddy river that ran parallel with the estuary before joining it at a break in the tall dunes. The *Ariadne* was the seventh boat along, a Liverpool Bay fisher, 39 feet long, 9 feet in the beam, which we had acquired and which we were doing up. In the *Ariadne* we were going to sail south one day. The master plan, according to Emlyn Rhys Morton.

The bow of the dinghy dug into the stinking black mud at the river's edge. I stepped aboard and Emlyn poled it out into the channel.

'I left my shoes on the front doorstep,' I told him.

'Marvellous,' he replied, 'bloody marvellous.' He settled in the stern, sculling with one hand. How did he manage to look so neat, so tidy – even after crawling all over that boat? Dirt didn't stay on him. He had clothes that didn't wrinkle. And it had always been like that. I had known him all my life.

'Don't rock the bloody boat,' I said.

'Got a bad head, matey?' He leered at me. 'Know what it means? Blood pressure! It'll probably kill you before you're thirty.'

'It's being so cheerful that keeps you going...'

'I'm talking facts. Your arteries are probably hardening prematurely. The next step is dizzy spells, then blackouts of increasing intensity, then a stroke. The long dive into oblivion; that's how you'll go. How many pints did you have?'

'It's the fags, not the beer,' I replied.

Emlyn laughed. 'Don't give me that. Heard it all before.' A great theorist, Emlyn Morton – especially on medical matters. 'Oh God my heart skipped a beat then! That's twice in the last hour. And I had the cramps last night – like a bloody contortionist in bed last night. Fucking killing ourselves – that's what we're doing.'

The dinghy bumped gently against the *Ariadne*'s hull. We climbed aboard. 'This old cow's not so well this morning, either,' he said. 'Had to pump her out. Leaking like a bucket down there.'

We sat on the roof of the cabin and surveyed the debris on the deck. Throughout the war the *Ariadne* had been on the beach, her planks shrinking, warping, parts of her looted by the town's beachcombers. We spent our days patching and caulking and painting, only to find new faults, new ruptures, new and rusty sores. 'No wonder they let us have her for fifteen quid,' Emlyn remarked, then added brightly, 'but we'll make something of her.' He stood and waved to a couple of fishermen as they rowed out to a mooring. Emlyn Morton was the most amiable character going. Always had been.

'Well,' he decided, 'we'll have to beach her tomorrow and give her a thorough going over.' He said it with relish. Another day of scraping and burning and caulking, the old boat propped up on that stinking, black mud.

But nothing got Emlyn Morton down. He had been like that at Jenkyn Pierce County School. I imagined that he had spent five years in the Air Force like that too. He was in a German camp for three of the years, but probably neat, composed, complaining mildly of his health and amiable even there. He'd picked up a Distinguished Flying Medal, although he wasn't sure what for and thought it didn't really matter anyway. They called his father the Rustler, because he had been, among other things, a dubious cattle dealer before he went bust. Only Emlyn and his father in that tall, dingy house in the Crescent now. A family that had known trouble. His mother, both his sisters dying of TB, and Idwal Morton half retired from life itself, a grey, remote man, full of shadows, with hands that trembled. Yet Emlyn came out of there each day fresh, alert, not a hair out of place, tiny and genial and with a smiling, school boy face.

We sat back and watched the gulls circle, the sun and the wind making new shades on the marram grass on the dune. I had dreamt of this place throughout the war, came home to it like a bee to a favourite flower, all the way from India... but now, after three weeks, we didn't talk about Bengal or Burma any more. No more talk of wars for us it was agreed. By the three of us. Mash – Marshall Trevor Edmunds – was our third man.

'Mind you, all this peace,' Emlyn said, 'gives you a right pain in the arse. Unless I've got piles of course. Anyway, what happened to you, after. Last night?'

'Morwenna Williams,' I said.

'Jesus H Christ! Nothing doing there, was there?'

'She said I was drunk...'

'You'd have to be. You should have stayed with us. Mash and me – we took over the band in that place.' He sniffed. 'Morwenna Williams – you must have been really desperate for it, mate.'

The town during the war had been lively with soldiers, a wide open place with girls chancing their luck. That's what I'd heard. But now uniforms gone, sobriety and settle down was the thing. All that warmth had cooled, all that giving had stopped.

'Thank God for Lilian,' I said. Lilian Ridetski, the ex-serviceman's standby, who didn't want to get married, who only knew one word and that was welcome; whom we shared, Emlyn Morton and me.

'Amen to that,' he said, then got to his feet. 'There's Mash now.' A giant in a lounge suit waving wildly from the mud bank before he ran, fully clothed, into that dirty, rubbish-strewn river and came swimming out to us, arms flailing, a wash behind him. We gave him a hand up over the side and he nearly had us over. He towered, dripping above us. A good suit that had been, a shirt that had been laundered white and stiff beneath it. There were green tendrils of seaweed on his County School tie.

'Guess where I've been?' he asked, a huge smile on his face.

'For a swim?' Emlyn suggested.

'No – to church,' Mash protested. 'Been with father to church!'

He stripped off and hung his clothes on the *Ariadne*'s rigging, and he lay down on the deck, a towel around his waist, and went to sleep. He had two scratches on one cheek, and a bruise under his left eye.

'After you'd gone,' Emlyn explained. 'Two punch-ups. Who with and what for, I haven't a clue.'

Mash had sat with us on the back row at school, and tried to keep up. Emlyn and I had scholarships, but Mash paid fees otherwise he wouldn't have been there at all. Then they pulled him out and found him a job as a solicitors' clerk – at the biggest solicitors in the country – but licking stamps and running errands was as far as he got. The army sent him to North Africa, later to Europe. In Germany he had been shot in the head by a British paratrooper who was drunk at the time, or it could have been in Holland by a German sniper or somewhere and someone else. Mash forgot. All the time and about everything. He had been waiting for me on the platform of Maelgwyn station when the train brought me home and Emlyn had to tell him who I was. He had all but crushed my hand with his grip.

'Will he mend, d'you think?'

‘So long as they don’t send him to any more bloody head doctors he’ll be all right,’ Emlyn replied.

‘Then why do they keep on pushing him? He’s always been thick – and they had him going in for exams and all that extra private tuition. And remember that business about making him a great athlete when it was plain to anybody that he might look the part but he’d got two left feet and no co-ordination.’

‘What do you expect with MT Edmunds for a dad?’ He drew his knees up under his chin. ‘We were a spell in Kent when we got back. I heard he was in this hospital near Bromley. Went over to see him. He could remember better then and it was a para who shot him. They got into an argument. This para pulls a gun and pops him in the head. Part of his brain went dead – and old MT Edmunds starts writing to the War Office for him to be mentioned in despatches!’

‘They just want to let him be,’ I said.

‘No chance. Remember when he got Moses and osmosis mixed up – those Christmas exams in form three? Every bloody question and he wrote “osmosis” for an answer!’ He laughed rocking himself gently as he did so.

The air was suddenly filled with the cries of children – a dozen or more of them charging up and down the dunes, shooting the daylight out of each other. ‘The trouble with the war,’ Emlyn said, ‘there weren’t any kids about – but this is all right isn’t it? We’ll get old *Ariadne* fit for the sea, and we’ll nudge her south, port by port to the Med, and we’ll find us a nice little harbour with white-washed houses behind on a hill and we’ll take out tourists and do a bit of fishing. All right?’

‘All right by me,’ I said. Mash snored gently, his

mouth wide open. 'So long as we don't have to work.'

Then we fell to discussing the local women and the danger of getting caught. And that led us to Lilian Ridetski and visits late at night, and the beauty of the arrangement, without a string attached.

'What happens if you're there when I call?' I asked him.

'I'll get off and let you in,' he replied, and went below to the cabin to practise his trumpet. He was good too. In his element in some smoky, dim-lit dance hall, giving the band a lift – but he usually complained afterwards about his lungs or his kidneys.

I lay back and thought of Lilian. Emlyn's discovery. She kept Maison Collette, Ladies High Class Hair Salon, in a little cul-de-sac off the High Street, and she lived alone above the shop. Ring at the door and a light comes on at the back of the shop. The door opens. Smell of scent and shampoo. 'Philip,' she says. 'Well, come in.' And the familiar ripple of a laugh to follow. 'What a surprise. Lovely.' She holds the door open, only wide enough for me to enter and I squeeze myself in and I have to brush against her and she catches hold, her mouth against mine, running her hand over the front of my trousers as she gently eases the door shut. No messing with Lilian. But she had trouble with names now and then.

'Oh, been out to those pubs again Harry?'

'Philip.'

'Excuse me!' And giggling up the stairs, the swish of her silk dressing gown ahead of me in the dark 'Philip, I meant!' Into a room with long velvet curtains and velvet cushions on the sofa piled high, and the tinkling of glass ornaments everywhere, and the spicy perfume, and the radio, and a pink shade masking the light. The nearest thing, in Emlyn's words, to a whore shop in Maelgwyn town.

Lilian, small and plump – 'something to grab hold of, eh?' – moves around on tip toes, playing at a little girl. Her eyes are brown and quick and she is all glances of invitation, daring you to touch and fondle. Her blonde hair is permed tight. 'Mind my hair,' she says. 'Don't want my hair messed up, see. Remember. Advert see.' A Polish name, but her accent is out of the Rhondda.

'Got time for a bit of cards, then?' It is the ritual. 'You sit there; I'll sit next to you.' Among the velvet cushions of the sofa. 'What's new, Philip?' Her short, soft fingers dealing out the cards. She chatters and makes jokes, double meanings everywhere, and sits even closer, warm flesh against my thigh, and she wins every hand in the game. Cheating I knew. 'Used to play strip poker in the old days. Used to play bridge too – only that was too clever for me, and Ridetski used to beat me when I overbid. With his fists I mean.' Ridetski, her husband, had been stationed at one of the camps near the town. She had come to Maelgwyn with him; wasn't a local. 'This old place – proper dead, isn't it? Mind you – might buck up again when the visitors come. Oh what a shame, Philip – you've lost again. What were you doing at my leg then? Felt you!'

She always wins the cards and the stake – half a crown. 'Oh poor Philip.' Her hand inside my shirt. The game abandoned, Lilian very playful, very expert. She opens her mouth wide to laugh, her tongue nudging at the side of her lips. A smooth, white throat. Ridetski walked out on her during the war. Was not expected back. 'Let's see.' She checks the score on the back of the envelope. 'Oh dear, Philip. Never mind. Now pay up. Pay up first.'

And once she has the coin in the palm of one soft hand, she lies back on the sofa and smiling all the time, pulls me towards her. Always on the wide sofa among the velvet cushions, never through in the bedroom. Her fingers digging into your back, all groans and giggles. Then she pushes you away, goes skipping to the bathroom, returning full of jokes and ready for more if you want it. A bit of slap and tickle. No demands, except one. Secrecy, or the promise of secrecy. 'No spreading anything around about me, hear. Got a nice little business.' Always that. And her winning the cards. She opens the door first, taking a glance about. 'Only cats around. Cats and naughty men who won't go home to bed. Come again won't you Philip?' And you leave her giggling and you walk home across the sleeping town, a distant sea breaking on a wide, empty beach, a siren or two for the waiting ships. Lilian Ridetski, a beautiful arrangement, not a string attached.

Emlyn flopped down beside me on the cabin top. He had spots before his eyes. Did I know that nobody in the whole of the medical profession had been able to explain those spots? He looked down at me. 'Hey – you been thinking about Lilian?'

'Does it show?'

'I'm psychic, young man. You went on Friday night, didn't you?'

'Where did Philip go on Friday night?' Mash was awake, crouching by the cabin, but even his torso seemed to fill the sky. 'Always talking about visiting. Who's this Lilian?'

'The ex–serviceman's best friend – bless her.'

'And all who sail in her,' Emlyn added.

Mash's flat face was blank and puzzled. 'I don't get it.'

'You can say that again!'

'But go on. Tell me.' He looked down at us, huge and pleading.

'Just a place to pop in and chat,' Emlyn said. 'A late night stop off.' Mash nodded, waiting for more.

'Maison Collette,' I said. 'Seen her haven't you?'

Mash beamed. 'That Mrs Ridetski? Mrs Lilian? Oh, yes, I've seen her.'

'Well then – that's where.'

'Her?' A grin split his face. 'She's all right that one. I'd say she was all right that Mrs Ridetski. Can I come?'

'Down, Rover,' Emlyn said.

'Ridetski,' Mash said. 'Some Welsh name...'

'What about Louise Gobrilmov?' Emlyn said. 'In form five, remember? She was Welshier than Owen Glendower.'

But Mash was not to be side-tracked. 'You'll let me join, all right?' He appealed to Emlyn, for him the leader in everything. Mash drew closer and touched Emlyn's shoulder. 'I'd like to join. I would.'

'Get your filthy hands off me,' Emlyn said, then he smiled. 'Not promising anything, mind – but we'll see what we can fix up. But no more swims in your Sunday best – OK?'

Mash gave a whoop, jumped high in the air, and the *Ariadne* rocked beneath us. 'Great!' he said. 'Isn't it a great day? "Summer's got a fine warm face".' He came out with this quotation now and then. The only one he knew, Emlyn claimed, just about the only thing that had stuck in his memory after all those years at school, all that private tuition. And what is more Emlyn was positive that the line came from a poem in the school magazine for 1937, a poem written by a boy in form two by the name of Edward Mortimer, whom I couldn't remember.

Emlyn remembered names and details that I had totally forgotten. Louise Gobrilmov – the family had been refugees from somewhere, and she a little dark girl with big eyes – but I only remembered the details through him. '"Winter has a cold embrace, Summer's got a fine warm face",' Mash said. And he nodded and smiled and flexed the huge muscles in his arms. 'I can join, can't I?'

'After you,' Emlyn said, 'she won't know we've been!' And we laughed and lay back, the day opening up around us, the fine warm face of summer above.

II

One step inside the Market Hall and you were in another age. Built by a speculator in Edwardian times it retained, after two wars, the atmosphere of those days. A step back in time to gas lighting, a penny bazaar look about the place. Around its perimeter were tiny lock up shops, in the centre open stalls for use on market days. All goods were on display because the shops had moveable shutters instead of windows, and there was a smell about the place – of fruit and meat and hung up leather shoes, and the public toilets – that was special, evocative. It had a sound of its own too – ringing, hollow, echoing – and the light in there was different from any other place in the town. Here my father had his bookshop, with which Laura now had to struggle. The wrong place, of course. Most of my father's ventures had been miscalculated.

That day when I had come back the other shopkeepers had given me a hero's welcome. From Mollie Ann Fruits to Isaac Moss Cobblers, from one end of the hall to the other they had come shuffling, first a wipe of the hand on a skirt or the backside of a trouser, then a firm grip. They were all elderly, all immensely dignified, all highly articulate. Rachel Boots and Shoes had even come forward with a verse, and Harry Morgan Second Hand Furniture had left a dead cert customer standing. Tom Parry Butchers had advised me to watch my health because your blood thinned in the tropics, and Nell Lewis Crockery had said, 'Well, I never, well I never' over and over again, just as she did when she watched the men having a piss in the gents. It was she and her sister Kate who had set up the mirror, their shop facing the urinals... Small traders, who had known my father, and who catered for bargain hunters and thin purses. I was glad to be in their company once again. But it was a hell of a place for a bookshop, a second-hand bookshop at that.

'Rushed off your feet, are you?' I asked Laura. She was sitting on a high stool outside the shop, a mug of tea on a pile of books, reading the *Daily Mirror.*

'My feet are perished,' she replied. That was something else about the Market Hall; it only had a few windows, and these were high up and black with years of grime, and so it was always cool in there, even in a heat wave. 'Ice box this old place,' she went on. On winter days she took a hot water bottle with her. That morning she had a paraffin lamp going.

'What time did you come in last night?'

'What time did you come in?' I countered, and she blushed.

'Told you I was going to the vestry to that social evening, didn't I?'

'That finished at nine,' I said. 'Who kept you out after that?' Laura Roberts, nearly ten years a widow, had a friend, a real man about town named William Wilkins, a bachelor and master baker and chapel deacon.

'None of your cheek,' she said, dimples in her face.

'I heard you come in. You fell down the stairs. Twice.'

'Was he up there with you? What did he say?'

She gave me a push. 'Oh be quiet – you and your dirty mind! You go and do that job for me and wash your tongue with caustic soda.' She clouted me with the *Daily Mirror.* 'Go on!'

Some of the shelving at the back of the shop had collapsed under the weight of books and she wanted it fixing. I edged my way around leaning towers of learned works that no one, surely to God, had read or would ever want to read. My father had followed every sale in the county and Laura too was still buying. 'You ought to ask the kids over on bonfire night,' I called out, and turned a corner around some sagging shelves and found myself looking at a real live customer. 'I was talking to Mrs Roberts,' I explained.

He snapped a book shut and stuffed it back on the shelf and gave me a dirty look. A tall, spidery old man, gold-rimmed glasses very low on an inflamed nose, a cigarette-yellow, gone-to-seed moustache. He had a trilby perched on his head and wore a black overcoat that was frayed at the cuffs, a scarf around his neck.

'Be so good as not to bellow,' he said, silver in his voice.

I swept books off a leaning shelf. The old man was muttering to himself. I banged a hammer under a shelf and went on banging; to hell with trade.

'I am looking for *The Historical Essays of Thomas Babington Macaulay,*' I heard him say.

'Ask Mrs Roberts,' I said as I aimed at a nail.

'Mrs Roberts has never heard of Mr Macaulay,' he snapped back. 'Haven't you got a catalogue?'

'No,' I said, and kept on banging. Maelgwyn was

littered with old men like him, spindle-legged old coots who had retired from business and who always looked tipsy with all that sea air. And this one I'd seen before, not getting enough kick from the ozone, dipping his nose into a glass of gin around the pubs. 'We've got bags of Bunyans if you're interested,' I told him.

'Ignoramus,' he growled, and reached for another book. There was a cigarette in his mouth now. He kept on flipping it against the tip of his long, hooked nose. Then taking it out had a coughing spell which sent him into a rage. He reached into his pocket and held out a card. 'Here laddie. *The Historical Essays of Thomas Babington Macaulay*. Can you remember that – Philip Roberts?'

I looked at the card. Didn't touch it. Just looked.

'Well take it; take it.' He had bright blue eyes, the eyes of a young man. I took the card. It said 'AMOS ELLYOTT', a London address crossed out and 'FLAT 2B OCEAN VIEW, MAELGWYN' written underneath. 'If you find it, bring it. Understood?' He stared, waiting for me to acknowledge.

'You'll be lucky,' I said and started hammering again.

He had to have the last word. 'I have been blessed with good fortune all my life,' he yelled at me, and whipping the scarf around his neck headed for the door.

When I had fixed the shelf, I went over to Laura and said, 'that old buzzard wants a copy of Macaulay's essays. Even wants them delivering. And he knows my name.'

'He called me a stupid woman,' Laura said. But Mash's father who had been talking to Laura thought that it was wonderful.

‘Marvellous man,’ he boomed, ‘but you know who he is surely? I have it on great authority; one of the nation’s great criminologists! He was, I am given to understand, an advisor to Scotland Yard,’ MT went on. Everyone called him MT: he insisted on it. MT stood for Meirion Trevor. MT stood for motor transport. And wasn’t that appropriate considering that he owned the finest, most up to date garage business on the coast? MT loved the superlative and was given to weak jokes. ‘Mind you,’ he’d say, ‘MT by name but not by nature.’

‘Amos Ellyott is a wonderful old man,’ he assured us. ‘A man of distinction. An asset to our town.’ MT was an enthusiast, quick to praise everything and everybody.

A tall man, though not as powerfully built as his son, he had Mash’s face, flat and broad, a tiny nose lost in the middle of it. He wore, invariably, a bow tie, and had a liking for suits of heavy tweed, often sporting a pair of plus fours – not a common sight in 1947. MT was the sporty gent who swept his way around the town, talking, enthusing, always on his way to a meeting somewhere.

‘One of the top men at the Yard, they say. We truly have some distinguished citizens don’t we Laura?’ He clutched at her arm which startled her. ‘But never mind about Mr Ellyott, Laura. What about these boys of ours? Aren’t they a great bunch? And having a whale of a time – up to all manner of misdemeanours – but fair play, Laura, fair play. Served King and country and by God they deserve it!’ He clapped a hand on my shoulder. ‘Philip – this old boat you’ve got. Having a smashing time on it, aren’t you?’

I had a feeling that I would always be ten years

old in MT's eyes. 'We've got to run her ashore this afternoon,' I said.

'I'd have a boat – well, if I were younger. But still I keep myself fit, off on the old run every morning.' He swept in closer. 'But what were you up to on Sunday morning? Never saw him in such a state.'

'Who's that?' Laura inquired.

'Marshall, that lad of mine. Comes home sopping wet, Laura! What were you up to? High jinks? A bit of wrestling and ducking eh?'

'You won't catch me wrestling with Mash...'

'Oh I bet! Oh dear me! But what did happen Philip? Did old Emlyn trip him up? Over he goes in the drink?'

'Missed his footing,' I said. 'He was getting out of the dinghy and he was in before we could catch him.'

'Ah – thought it would be something like that.' He sounded relieved. 'These boys of ours, Laura – they're a caution.' He removed his gold watch from his pocket. 'Well, look at the time. I must be bustling... Good morning to you both. Philip – you must come to the house. See my good lady. Don't forget!' He waved his hat at us, then went charging into the gloom of the Market Hall, greeting each shopkeeper in turn.

'The human dynamo,' I said.

Laura looked past me at someone and pulling her purse out of her overall pocket. 'End of the month,' she whispered. 'Here comes the moneylender.'

George Garston believed in looking poor. A shirt without a collar helped, so did an old, patched jacket and a pair of cord trousers at half mast. But even in a suit from Savile Row, he would have looked poor and hangdog and furtive. Sallow skinned, he was always in need of a shave. There was a smell of wet ferrets about him and something ferret-like in his approach.

'Morning missus.' A quick glimpse of yellowed teeth.

Laura treated him to silence, a sure sign of distaste with her. She held out the money. He wrote in his book with the stub of a pencil, the owner of Market Hall collecting his rents. They said he had property all over town, more property than anyone knew.

'Home for good now, Philip?' he said without looking at me.

'That's right, Mr Garston. When's your David due for demob?'

I said it to annoy. It did, too. 'David is at a London University studying for his doctor's examinations.' Only a brief fight in him, then the whine was back in his voice. 'Got rejected for his medical, see – with his chest.' He took the money and shuffled away, one shoulder sagging.

Laura shivered. 'Always feel like having a good wash when he's been.'

After that I helped her sort out yet another tea chest full of books which she had bought blind from an auction.

'The way we're going,' I said, 'we'll have to take the bird man's shop next door.' The bird man had gone bust, the shop empty now. There was a stairway at the back of that shop, the only way up to the top floor of the Market Hall. The top floor was identical with the ground floor, but never opened now, never used. Still, the Hall was a handy place for a bringing a girl on a wet night. All dry places had to be noted and remembered. I had already tried our shop with a girl named Susan

Todd, and she had gone home crying because a set of *The Children's Encyclopaedia* had fallen on her head.

Laura said, 'You didn't tell the truth about his son – MT's son – about how he got wet, did you? Is he having trouble that boy?'

'Not so you'd notice it,' I said, and suddenly I remembered that day, long before the war, a hot stifling day, and I was in our backyard, and the gate had swung open, and there stood Mash. In both hands he held a viper, tail flicking, and he was saying 'this one's bit me twice!' My father came running from the house and made him drop the snakes on the stone floor, and his heel came down on their heads, and Mash stood there crying. All at once I remembered that... A boy with vipers. His arm came up like a balloon that night. We went to visit him, Emlyn and I.

'Wounded in the head, wasn't he?' Laura was saying. 'I saw you shiver then.'

And I said I must have been thinking about old George Garston, man of property, who had come on a fair pace during the war to end all wars.

The Crescent had been the best part of town a long time ago, a terrace of substantial, three-storey houses with steps leading up to the front doors and neat, protective railings all along. But it had, in Laura's words, gone down, the richer moving out to newer properties along the front and less successful people moving in. It backed on to the railway line, seemed to lean forward over the street. The railings had gone to the war effort and the houses were naked and exposed as a result. A downcast street now, limp grey curtains behind the windows and woodwork yelling for paint. Emlyn's house especially so. I remembered the Mortons in brighter surroundings, a spacious white house with flower beds and shrubs, a pony named Scouser in the paddock, but that was before Idwal Morton's fortune had taken a dive.

He opened the front door for me. 'Come through to the morning room,' he said. 'Will you look at this place? Christ. I'd sort it all out if only I knew where to start.' He removed a pile of newspapers from a chair and told me to sit. We were in the kitchen at the back of the house, smell of old food in the air, the sink cluttered with crockery.

He had an *Express* spread out on the table, a pencil in his hand. The pencil shook. 'Studying form. Don't back anything. Just what you might term a hobby.' He looked at the print through a magnifying glass, squinting, lines fanning upwards across his huge forehead to the crown of his bald head. A grey wasted man who gave the impression he'd forgotten you were there. But as a boy I had always liked him, probably because he was like that, didn't fuss, didn't go in for head-patting. A two-bottle-a-day man, the know-alls said, but not any more. Idwal Morton, an old grey cardigan over his shoulders, had retired into long silences broken only by small, ironic remarks. 'Help yourself to the killers,' he said, indicating the cigarettes.

Emlyn came in. He was wearing his demob suit, an identical pattern to mine, only he had found a better fit. 'Here I am father – all ponced up,' he said. Idwal snorted. 'Has father been entertaining you, Philip?'

'Oh – Philip knows me, Emlyn,' Idwal said. 'By the way, I'm going to melt down that bloody trumpet of yours while you're out.'

'The neighbours will give you a medal,' Emlyn said. At the front door he whispered to me, a smile on his face. 'That's the first time he's spoken to me today. You've no idea how rowdy this house is.'

We took a short cut to the High Street and grinned at each other when we saw a woman come out of Maison Collette, a silk scarf covering her hair. 'As a matter of fact I called last night,' Emlyn said. 'A chat and a coffee...'

We then had to dive down an alley to avoid the Reverend Price who was sailing towards us. Ministers and local girls were in the same boat as far as we were concerned: intent on settling us down. We didn't return to the subject of Lilian until we were on the promenade.

'Facts are facts,' Emlyn said, 'and the biggest fact of all is that Mash has got the urge.'

'Perhaps he'll forget about it.'

'Not this... Oh Christ, slow down for God's sake – think of my health. No, no – this is the old primeval urge. This no memory can erase. And besides, it's a question of mates.'

'Ok. We share his car, we share the boat, we share fags and money, we share all the lousy bints we pick up at the lousy dances. So now we've got to share Lilian Ridetski?'

He gripped my arm and drew me to a halt. 'You don't mind do you? Because if you do – say so.' An anxious look on his face, but I knew Emlyn Morton of old. He was the arranger, always had been. His mind already made up, a course of action planned, but now there had to be an agreement, everything sorted out neat and tidy. If you've got any objections Philip, we'll take them into consideration – and carry on with the plan he devised in the first place.

'I don't mind – but what about Lilian?'

We walked on. 'Well – to tell you the truth I did make some preliminaries…'

'You do surprise me.'

'Don't be like that. A little dash of Lilian might very well help Mash along.'

'Been very helpful to us,' I agreed. 'You take him round; you introduce him.'

We were level with one of the small, pagoda-like shelters that dotted the promenade when a voice called out urgently. 'Young men! I am in some distress.'

It was Amos Ellyott, sitting there in the shelter, a silver-knobbed stick between his legs. He looked all right to me.

'An arrogant old bugger,' I whispered to Emlyn. 'Leave him be.' But Emlyn went up to him and offered assistance.

'I am locked,' Amos Ellyott said angrily. 'My joints have seized. Kindly straighten me.' Emlyn at once got hold of his elbow and tried to lift him. 'Both sides!' the old man barked. I joined Emlyn and we raised him to his feet, where he then ordered us to let go as he took a few tentative steps.

'Don't forget my book, Roberts. Your friend's name?'

'Emlyn Morton,' Emlyn said.

'I am Ellyott. Help him find the *Macaulay*. Don't forget.'

We watched him walk away as if he was facing a high wind. 'Arrogant old sod,' I said. 'What about a thank you then?'

But Emlyn liked him straight away. 'Pissed as a fart,' he said admiringly. 'A detective, wasn't he?'

'The trouble with you,' I told him sourly, 'is you like everybody.'

We were on our way to Mash's for tea and the villas now were spacious and far removed from each other. They had, more often than not, names on their gate posts of places where the owners had made a pile. Solihull and Kidderminster. MT's house was called The Grange. A house belonging to MT was bound to be called that.

Mash and MT were playing tennis when we arrived. MT wore a pair of shorts that came well below the knee, and he was stained with sweat and out of breath. 'You've just missed the championships,' he panted. 'And this is the champion himself.' He held up Mash's huge arm. 'By three clever sets – but not without a fight! Come on, I'll race you to the house – last one stinks!'

Mash took him on. They handed us their racquets, then went scampering up the short drive, reached the front door at the same time and jostled and charged each other as they crashed into the house.

As we followed them in, I wondered who was running the garage on such an afternoon as this. But, as everyone knew, the money came from MT's wife. It was her house too.

She was waiting for us in the big room at the back, a tall, severe looking woman with sparse hair and horn–rimmed glasses. Never a beauty, I'd heard people say, and it was her money that had got her MT, wasn't it? So much I'd forgotten in five years.

She rose from her chair to greet us. 'Tenth time I've asked that boy to tell you to come.' She gave us a stiff handshake. 'He forgets, doesn't he?'

'Something like that,' Emlyn said. He was much better at small talk than I was.

We sat in silence and listened to the howls upstairs as MT and Mash fought over the bathroom. Through the window I could see swallows flitting low over the trim lawns; Mrs Edmunds knitted. We were there as Mash's friends, not because she liked us.

'Have you started work,' she asked Emlyn suddenly.

'Percy Davies Auctioneers has come round offering me my old job back,' Emlyn replied. 'And an enormous salary, of course. I'm giving it my full consideration.'

She didn't smile. 'You were in the sixth form at school, Philip – when you were called up? You both should try for the university. Both of you clever.'

I caught the bitterness in her voice, and wondered why she had to be so sour, until I remembered that she had Mash as a problem.

Tea time proved to be a conversation between Emlyn and MT. But mainly MT.

'These boys, Sylvia! Aren't they cases? Back home again where they belong, painting the town red and messing about with that old boat.'

Mrs Edmunds poured the tea, pretending she'd heard nothing.

'Stay around here, is my advice. We're going to make it the town it was before the war.' He pointed a knife at all of us in turn. 'Revive, that's the motto! Open the tennis courts; start the tournaments again. And there's the golf club, crying out for members. And the old football team – remember?'

Photographs came out of his wallet and were passed around. 'We'll clean up our beautiful beach, the old yacht club on its feet again. And the people will be crowding off the trains. I've got the carnival committee going again. It won't be much this year, but it'll be a start. And the sports day – remember the sports day? You, Philip, I remember you winning the egg and spoon!'

I couldn't. When Emlyn, or MT now, spoke of something I had done as a boy I kept wondering why I hadn't remembered without their prompting.

The telephone rang. Mrs Edmunds went to answer it and came back to say, tight lipped, 'That Garston – for you.' Making Garston sound like a disease, speaking to MT without looking at him.

Mash, Emlyn and I were in the trophy room, when he returned. 'That old Garston,' he explained, 'been chasing me for a car for his son.' His face was more ruddy than usual, and he seemed nervous, agitated. He went towards the window, and looked out. 'You know – you can't touch this place, can you? I couldn't be anywhere else but here. In this town.' MT turned, laughing to himself. 'Sentimental, that's what I am.'

In the evening we climbed into Mash's car and drove to the Ferryman's Arms down the coast, where there was a dance. A flat affair with only two likely candidates, and both of them had husbands in tow.

Emlyn turned to Mash, 'now is the hour,' he said. Mash understood straight away. He had us back in Maelgwyn by eleven. I left them on the High Street, and went home smiling.

III

I was looking after the shop for Laura when Emlyn arrived with the news. 'A tremendous success,' he told me, doing a fair imitation of MT. 'Marvellous. Woke me up this morning to tell me about it. Wants me to teach him the cards!'

'He knows how to play...'

'Yes – but he can't understand why he lost every hand.'

'Anything else to report?'

'Nothing that you could make sense of. But I am prepared, on the evidence of physical scrutiny alone, to sign affidavits that all went according to plan...'

'What did she say, when you took him in?'

He began to peer along the shelves, running his finger along the spines of the books. 'I introduced him. She said 'fancy'. I said this young man requires a modicum of therapeutic manipulation...'

'Oh, bollocks!'

'The truth, my friend. I'm a dab hand at that kind of thing, coming as I do from a long line of brothel owners. Leads me to wonder if we shouldn't open our own whorehouse when we get to foreign parts in the boat.'

'They usually have a Madame,' I said.

'I could always wear a skirt – and I'll slap you with my handbag if you don't take that look off your face!'

He went into the shop, following the titles all the way. 'So what happens now?'

'Mash? He's going again tonight!'

'Great! You've done for the two of us now, haven't you? What the hell are you looking for, anyway?'

'He'll get tired of it. In any case, we can always work shifts. Nothing will change.'

'You and your fucking theories. What are you looking for?'

'That Macaulay book – for the old man.'

'For him? Arrogant old sod like that?'

'Fascinates me,' Emlyn said. 'The trouble with you is people don't fascinate you – so you've no chance of being a fascinator like me.'

Laura came in at that point to report a disturbance, and asked for us to take a look, but not to get involved. It was market day, most of the stalls with produce or goods on display, and more business than any other days, in spite of the ration books and coupons. The disturbance was taking place around a stall run by a second-hand clothing merchant named Gareth Ince.

'It's that German man he's got working for him,' Laura said. 'The trouble's to do with him.'

The German was a toothless ex-Prisoner of War, a fat, bald man, turnip faced, with tiny porcine eyes. He had elected to stay behind, living off odd-jobs.

When we reached the crowd Mollie Ann Fruits was ordering Jack Partridge to put him down. 'Everybody has the right to live in peace,' she was saying, her sentiments having no effect at all on Jack.

The Partridge lot were notorious pub fighters, a

host of them, their real name was Williams, but they were called Partridge because a grandfather had once run a pub of that name. Wife-beaters all of them, and patriotic to a fault. Jack Partridge was wearing his medal ribbons on his jacket.

'This Nazi swindled me,' he roared.

'When did you ever have any money to be swindled,' Mollie Ann inquired.

'Piss off, woman,' Jack told her, and gave the German a shake. The German's face was puce.

'Short changed me in the Bull last night,' Jack growled. The German helped out in a number of pubs. 'The bloody Nazis are taking our boys' jobs.'

'When did you start worrying about jobs?' shouted Mollie Ann.

'All Nazis should be hung,' Jack said. Then he hit the German on the mouth. I hadn't expected him to do that and the crowd backed away. They were looking to Emlyn and me, trained fighting men. A trickle of blood ran down the German's chin. He made no effort to fight back, suspended there like a great balloon.

But Mollie Ann stepped in smartly and rapped Jack across his kidneys. He dropped the German and went for her, and she skipped out of reach and took refuge behind us.

'Oh my God, will you look at him?' Emlyn whispered. 'My blood pressure's soaring.'

Jack came closer. I could smell booze on him. I was going to have to take him: him or me, I thought grimly.

But Emlyn was clutching at my hand. 'Maybe we ought to retire to discuss tactics,' he suggested. 'Tell him we were on his side,' Emlyn was saying as we were thrust aside and Jack was faced with someone much bigger than us, and what he saw made him blink and stagger back.

'What's up then?' Mash inquired.

Jack took on a beaten look and decided that the opposition was too great and went stumbling off through the crowd. The women rushed past us to tend to the German.

'Thank God you came along,' I said to Mash.

He stood there staring at the German who was now having tea poured down him and panting '*danke,* miss, *danke*'.

The door to the bird man's shop next to ours was ajar. It seemed only right that we should have a look in, a natural progression to climb the stairs at the back, the only access to the top storey of the Market Hall.

It was many years since I had been up there, and it was after all only a repeat of the ground floor – lock up shops, a space in the centre for stalls. This was another of the town's great failures, to be included with a hundred-bedroom hotel, a disaster of a sea wall, building and development projects had come to grief. Here the fault was obvious; the architect had forgotten to include a public staircase in his plans.

The top floor was ill-lit from a number of skylights now filmed with soot, but there was light enough to see the junk strewn about once we were in the open space. I had no memory of rows of tip up wooden chairs, all of them facing a white rectangle on the far wall. But there had been talk of picture shows, hadn't there? Big plans that had been scotched by fire regulations. Emlyn's hand tightened on my arm. There was a man sitting on the front row of chairs. Mash sneezed. The man turned and rose to face us. It was George Garston.

He came down the aisle between the chairs, a curious limping walk, waving a notebook at us. 'Now then, now then – not allowed. Trespassers will be prosecuted.' The voice he used to scare the local children from the fields around his farm. 'Clear off! This is private property!' We weren't children any more. We didn't move. And as he came closer and recognised us his manner changed. 'Oh – you is it? Marshall and Philip.'

'And me,' Emlyn said.

Garston stuffed his notebook in his pocket. 'I know you all of course. I suppose you thought you'd have a look? Nothin' much to see up here, is there? Just old rubbish gathering dust. I have to come up here now and then, to make sure everything's all right, but there's nothing worth taking is there?' The poor man now, the blind beggar.

'Then why don't you give it away?' Emlyn asked him.

Garston avoided the question. 'Get Marshall to tell his father I am waiting for news of the car.'

Mash hadn't been listening. 'Tell him what?' he said, then walked over to examine one of the shops, peering through the shutters.

George Garston drew closer to us. 'I hear he's in a bad way,' he whispered, jerking a long, black thumbnail in Mash's direction.

'You hear wrong,' Emlyn said.

'But – a bullet in his head, that's what I heard...'

'Bullshit.' Emlyn's voice quiet but hard.

'Well – it's only what I heard. His father's very worried.'

'You're thinking of someone else,' Emlyn said.

Then, in a voice that was tight and harsh, firing off each phrase, 'Mash is all right. Cured. Nothing wrong with him at all. Just stories they push around the town. Got that?' He waited for Garston to nod. 'It's just gossip, a bit like your David.'

'What d'you mean, my David?' Garston snapped.

'Well, that's only gossip too, about him drinking every night in the King's Arms.'

'You are mistaken!' Real anger in Garston's voice. 'Every night he's at home preparing for the exams. You are mistaken.'

'Like you about Marshall Edmunds?' Emlyn suggested, and he gave me the nudge and called Mash over and left George Garston with his empire.

Outside the Hall in the sunshine Emlyn said, 'Fancy me telling tales like some old woman.' I was third man where Emlyn and Mash were concerned: always had been. Emlyn cheerfully referred to Mash as an old nut case, but no one else was allowed to do so. Not even me. 'Now what shall we do tonight?' And we looked at Mash and laughed.

But Mash went every night for a week and I had occasion to fling Emlyn's words in his face. Until, out of the blue, came Dawn and Shirley, on holiday from an insurance office in Liverpool and looking for a good time. Emlyn and I took them out most afternoons and every night, and work on the *Ariadne*, still propped in the mud, went slowly.

'Mind you,' Emlyn said from a reclining position on the *Ariadne's* deck, 'we'll have to set to. Soon as these two dollies go home.' We lay there on the top deck. Emlyn inhaled deeply. 'My God, doesn't this old river pong? Two lungfulls and you've got typhoid.' He leaned over on one elbow. 'Tell you what though, I wish we could find a couple of rich dollies, who'd look after us!'

'We're all right for the time being,' I said. 'Everything's for the time being.'

Mash bellowed from below. 'Is there only me working?' A few minutes later he appeared, such enormous shoulders, such a small head by comparison. In order to cover the scar Mrs Edmunds had insisted that he let his hair grow, and now it was thick and curly. He had tar on his face, on his chest, on his arms, as he swung over the side and came towards us we could see the harbour mud had given him a pair of black socks and we laughed. He crouched in front of us, frowning, his mouth in a pout. A boy's face still.

'You're doing a great job, Mash boy,' Emlyn told him. 'Just you take a breather.'

Emlyn began to sing to himself as he lay back taking in the sun. Usually Mash could never resist joining in, but that day he was silent, staring blankly into the distance. I wondered what he was thinking; how he thought. Then suddenly, as if he had made up his mind about something, he crawled over and knelt between us. 'I want to ask you,' he began, 'something.' Mash closed his eyes so tight that a vein appeared on his forehead. 'You don't go, do you?'

That was all he said, but we knew what he meant. A conversation with Mash was a matter of making the right assumptions.

'How the hell can we go when you're there all the time?' I said.

Emlyn's elbow jarred approvingly against my ribs. 'You're flying solo, old boy.'

Mash's face seemed to light up. 'Honest?'

'Look mate, we've got these two girls to see to,' Emlyn confirmed.

'We don't go, honest,' I said.

'But she calls me Philip sometimes – or Emlyn.'

'That's part of the gag,' Emlyn said.

'It's no gag!' Mash banged his fist on the cabin roof.

'Well – she makes a mistake. Anybody can make a mistake.'

A silence fell, Mash's lips moving but no words coming out.

'For fuck's sake Mash, how could we go? Me and Philip – we've got plenty on our hands...'

'Yes – but I don't want you to go no more!' The words exploded out of him. Suddenly he looked away. 'Don't want you two to go no more.' The line of his jawbone was set tight. 'It's what I mean.' He shook his head. I could see the scar beneath his hair.

'Is that all?' Emlyn said. 'Well – it's all right by us, isn't it Philip?'

'But you've got to promise! Promise now. Now.'

He looked at each of us in turn, deep-set eyes, opaque, anxious. 'You've got my word,' I said.

'Me too,' Emlyn added. 'Honest.'

'Honest?' Mash's face broke into a huge smile. We both nodded. Emlyn punched him gently on the chest. 'Great then.' Mash leapt to his feet and did a handstand above us, lowering himself expertly to the deck. 'I'll get some work done, then,' he said, kicking the soles of our feet. 'Idle buggers!'

He climbed over the side. Emlyn looked at me.

'You and your theories,' I said.

Dawn and Shirley caught a train back home and we became questing men about pubs and dances once more. Mash was always with us, but only until a certain hour. He was much brighter, we thought, less inclined to fight.

One night we met Amos Ellyott, all alone in the saloon bar of the King's Arms, and three parts cut. It was a Tuesday night, no parties to crash, no dances, all the girls at home washing their hair. I was about to do a smart about turn at the sight of Amos, but Emlyn headed straight for him, and offered to buy him a drink.

'I never pay for drinks,' he explained, 'I am a good cause. They have appeals on my behalf.'

'Catch him when he falls off the stool,' I whispered to Emlyn.

'I heard that!' The old man said. 'I have superb hearing. And I am rude and overbearing because society allows me to be.'

'This is a great ending to a great evening,' I said, and he heard that as well, and went on talking. He knew all about us, had seen us in the company of the giant; young men home from the war. He knew all about Dawn and Shirley and where we lived, all about our families.

'Your father,' he said to Emlyn, 'is known as the Rustler. The nick–name is everything in tiny towns, is it not? But only among the true natives, not among the nameless new-comers, all these little old women, all these little old men who have come here for the express purpose of dying.'

At that moment he fell off his stool, and the barman asked us to take him home. I was all for leaving him, but Emlyn insisted we do the right thing.

We propped him up and marched him to Ocean View, to the door of his flat. And all the time he talked. He had three honorary degrees; he was the author of learned works; his obituary notice in *The Times* had already been written. 'The key's above the door,' he said. 'Take me in, settle me down.'

The room had nearly as many books as my father's shop, most of them open, as if he read a line here, a line there. A good stock of empty bottles too. We planted him in a chair, tugged off his boots and propped his feet up on a stool.

Emlyn brought a blanket from the bedroom, and as he spread it over him he sang:

You have a kind face you old bastard,
You ought to be bloody well shot;
You ought to be tied to a lamppost,
And left there to bloody well rot!'

Amos Ellyott giggled helplessly. 'Thank you kind boys,' he said, 'and thank you for the *Macaulay*.' He was snoring as we went out.

'What made you take him the book?' I said when we reached the street.

'Found a copy of it at home. Least I could do. They've got the old bugger's obituary notice written...'

'The trouble with you,' I said, 'is that you're too bloody pleasant.'

There was a mist down, already an occasional bray from the sirens of the big ships out in the estuary.

'It's a mortuary this place,' I said. We sat on a bench on the promenade, the mist forming around us, and Emlyn talked about smoky clubs and night people and coloured lights and music.

Not everyone in Maelgwyn had settled down for the night. Out of the mist, dressed in a polo necked sweater and shorts, MT Edmunds came running.

'Philip, Emlyn, how wonderful!' He was running on the spot as he talked. 'I'm killing two birds with one stone!' He showed us a bundle of posters. 'Keeping fit and spreading the word. The revival of the town! The Carnival day, the Sports Day – a poster on every lamp post. We don't expect anything too brilliant this year, but no matter. To begin is enough.' And he went on like that, and I remembered someone saying that MT was thick as two short planks and that even his wife had stopped feeding money into the business.

'Must be off,' he cried out. 'Like fire in the lungs, this air. Good night to you boys!' He went off at a sprint.

'He never asked about Mash,' Emlyn said. 'I wonder if word's getting around?'

'Keeping an eye on the situation, you mean?'

'Could be. My dad says that business is running down. My dad says that old Georgie Garston is all set to buy MT out.'

'Knows everything, your dad.'

Emlyn laughed. 'That's why the old bugger went bankrupt.'

Tuesday night, the dead night of the week. Made for a visit to Lilian and her soft, fat fingers dealing out the cards. But that wasn't possible any more.

IV

Mash had an arm lock on Emlyn's neck. He was swinging him around above the black mud. Emlyn's face was purple, his eyes staring, glazed. There was blood on them both, and I stood there and did nothing.

That day we had all been taken with a need for work and applied ourselves to the *Ariadne.* I was up on deck, caulking yet another seam. I could hear them chatting below me on the mud, and I was thinking how close they had always been, a private understanding between them. And I heard a shout, sounds of a struggle, and thought that Emlyn had started ragging about. There was a long silence, broken only by the sound of heavy breathing, and I went over the side to look.

It was minutes before I realised what was happening. And all I could do was shout, 'Hey Mash! For Christ's sake put him down! You're killing him!'

I grabbed Mash's arm and tried to break the lock. His muscles were steel hard. I kicked at his shins. 'Let go you stupid bastard!' I hit him in the kidneys, as hard as I could, and he grunted and sent me sprawling with one sweep of his free hand. I picked myself up off the mud and went skidding back to them. Emlyn was still conscious, kicking and jabbing at Mash without any effect. 'For fuck's sake, Mash, put him down!'

Mash's eyes were closed. I saw the muscle on his arm bulge as he tightened his grip. Then I had this old stick in my hands. God knows where it came from. It was there under the seaweed and I had it in my hands, and I was telling Mash I'd brain him. Emlyn's legs went limp. I aimed for the tip of Mash's elbow, gave it all I had and felt the sting of the blow in my hands. Mash gave a great howl and dropped Emlyn, and I stood facing him, swinging the stick, waiting.

He had one hand clamped on his elbow. 'Oh Jesus, oh Jesus,' he was saying. He sank to his knees still saying it. Then in a broken voice, added, 'Philip – what did you do that for?'

I tossed the stick aside and knelt by Emlyn and turned him over. There was blood coming from his nose. I saw his eyelids flicker and raised him to a sitting position and held his head between his knees.

Mash was at my side, full of concern. 'What happened to him, Philip? What happened to Emlyn?'

I sent Mash to the river to fetch some water. He came back with a bucketful and I set to work on Emlyn's face. He came round quickly, retching and spluttering. 'Jesus Christ, that's salt water,' I heard him say, and I felt better. I told Mash to get up to the cabin and put a kettle on the stove for some tea. 'Yes, Philip,' he said, like a child pleased at being sent on an errand.

'What the fuck happened?' Emlyn had a coughing spell and did a great deal of spitting. He held both his hands around this throat. 'Oh, shit!' he said in a croaking voice, said it again and again.

'He nearly had you...'

'You don't have to tell me.'

'What started it? Were you fooling about or what?'

He drew a long, ragged breath into his lungs and slowly heaved himself to his knees. 'We were working just there.' He pointed to a patch at the bow of the boat. 'We were chatting, singing a bit.' I helped him to his feet. 'Shit! There wasn't an argument, even.'

'You didn't say anything to get him mad?'

'How the hell can I remember? We were just chatting. When suddenly he goes for me. Throws a punch and catches me here.' He touched the pulped skin above his ear. 'I didn't even go back at him.'

'You didn't say anything – you're sure?'

He shook his head. 'Philip?' Again the appeal. 'He just went for me. Did you ask him?'

'Doesn't know what happened,' I said. I told him about the stick. We stood there for a while just looking at each other, then I helped him up the ladder.

In the *Ariadne*'s cabin Mash was pouring boiling water into the mugs. I told him to put tea in first, and he blushed and said 'Oh hell – I forgot.' Then we sat, Mash and I on one side, Emlyn on the other. Mash talked, even quoted the line about "Summer's warm face", and I kept asking myself how he could forget so easily. Emlyn was slumped on the seat, streaks of mud, blood on his face and chest, trying to sip the tea and finding it painful to swallow. And Mash there, as if he didn't notice, as if Emlyn always looked like that.

'When I was in the unit,' Mash said brightly, 'we used to say roll on demob – every day. Roll on fucking demob. Roll on fucking demob – every day.' His round, firm jaw twitched as he searched for more words. A silence fell over the cabin. I could hear the gulls outside.

'OK, you all right now?' I asked Emlyn.

'Except that I've been through the mangle,' he croaked.

Then Mash spoke up again. 'We were away when it happened. There was this man who was burnt to death on the coast road there. You heard about it?'

How had it got onto that tack, I wondered. 'Yeah, some Yank,' I said, 'up on Morwyn Hill. Car he was in caught fire.' Why the hell were we talking about this?

'You heard about it, Philip? Where was I then?' He shook his head. I remembered Laura sending me a cutting from the local paper about it. Oh shit – would he go for Emlyn again? Would there be a stick next time? 'But Philip – you see he was burnt to death in pound notes,' Mash went on eagerly. 'He had this car and it was full of pound notes. Now – that's a fact. Burnt to death in pound notes!'

'Oh Christ,' Emlyn sighed. 'Philip – I have to go. Got to get some air by myself.' He slid along the seat then ducked his head as he went out. We heard the pad of his shoes on the deck above us, then silence. When I went out on deck he was walking in the black mud at the river's edge, shoulders hunched.

Mash said, 'In pound notes, Philip. Burnt in pound notes.'

'Come on Mash,' I said, knowing even then that it was hopeless, 'what the fuck were you doing? Why did you go for him like that?' And all he did was look at me, a flat, blank look. Was it possible for someone to be like that? 'Oh come on,' I said, 'let's get some work done.'

We worked together all afternoon, and he broke into song every now and then. The day shone like a pearl. You could see the little town from the river, sleeping there among the sand hill. Nothing changed whilst I had been away. Except the people. I looked at Mash. Had he attacked me it would have made sense.

I was the third man, never as close... Unless – it was a piercing thought – Emlyn had paid Lilian a visit and Mash had seen him or heard about it.

'Philip – did Emlyn fall?' Mash squatting on the deck. 'I must have fallen as well. Seen my elbow?'

'The fact of the matter,' Laura said, 'is the shop's only just paying its way...'

'All right,' I said, 'I'll get a job.'

'You write off for one of them grants for college. Like Mr Wilkins says...'

We were having a mug of tea outside the shop and the conversation was about normal for that time of day. Across the Hall I could see the German at his stall, a crowd around him, one of the attractions – he was lately the enemy.

'Think about it,' Laura advised. She was a good looking woman still, and lumbered with me.

'You marry Will Wilkins, that's the solution.'

'Oh, get lost,' she replied, embarrassed yet pleased. She lifted her feet and examined her shoes. 'Are you trying to get rid of me, boy?'

'We could get rid of him, after he's made his will...'

'Oh, terrible you are. Awful.'

Ceri Price, who had been with me at school, walked up at that moment.

'I was telling him he's awful,' Laura said to her.

'He always was,' Ceri said. A small, quiet girl at school, but most definitely blossoming now. 'My father's mad for a book of poems by Yeats – he gets these fancies.' Her father was the local reporter, known as Price the Scoop. He was a poet too.

I took Ceri into the shop, Laura giving me a knowing

wink, and I learnt that she was studying the piano in London and term had just finished, and that's why I hadn't seen her around. I had a date for the pictures, outside the Regal at 7.30, in no time at all, and I rejoiced as I stood with Laura and watched her walk away.

'Hasn't she got lovely eyes?' Laura said. 'And her hair – just like a film star.' I didn't correct her. Laura loved the pictures, but Will Wilkins wasn't so keen. She liked a glass of stout too, but he was a strict teetotaller. 'You wouldn't really want me to marry again, would you?'

'Like that, is it?'

She blushed like a young girl. 'I've got a feeling I may be asked, that's all.' Then she got flustered and picked up her handbag and headed for the Ladies – a place she never used...

'You took Ceri Price to the pictures?' Emlyn said. 'My God, come and join us! Anything doing?'

'I never tried.'

'As bad as that? Have another pint. You can pay. I'm using the Amos Ellyott system.' We were in the King's Arms, our favourite pub. It was Friday night, the doors and windows open wide, a summer wind coming in off the estuary. Emlyn was wearing a silk scarf to hide the bruising on his throat. He had dispensed with the plaster above his ear. He looked dapper, like something off the fag adverts.

'Three pints of best bitter,' I said, placing the drinks on the table. 'Hey where are you off to?' I asked Mash.

Mash pointed silently to the gents. I took the chance to ask Emlyn how they had got on that day.

'Fine,' he replied. 'Everything's OK.' He raised his glass and drank.

'Yes, but what did Mash say? Did you talk it out with him?' There was no response from Emlyn. 'I asked you a bloody question.'

He placed his elbows on the table, cupped his face in his hands. 'Not the real question, though, was it?'

'What d'you mean?'

'What you want to know is did Mash go berserk because he saw me coming out of Lilian's,' he grinned. A challenge on the table, and I was about to take it up when he said, 'Oh God, look who's here.'

MT came sweeping in, called four pints as he passed the bar and planted himself at our table.

'Hasn't it been a wonderful day?' he said. 'Marvellous! Absolutely marvellous. Like the summers of old. We can only pray' – he looked up at the ceiling – 'that it holds for carnival week.' The sun had left blisters on his forehead. 'The first step back on the road to recovery.' The barman placed four pints on the table. 'Thought I'd join you for a little session,' he said, and cleared the best part of his pint in a couple of noisy gulps.

'Didn't know you were a drinking man,' Emlyn said.

'It used to be fifteen pints a night back in the old rugger days.' He gave Mash a friendly punch as he rejoined us. 'My God, I've sunk some stuff in my time. You boys – drink? You've no idea...' and he went rambling on about the times he'd had, and calling out for more pints from the bar. Emlyn and I had them lined up, but Mash who had the bigger capacity kept up with him and seemed to be the only one who was listening to him too. 'We used to drink the bars dry. But never mind about ancient history...'

'Hear, hear,' Emlyn said.

'Now is what counts. There's going to be a renaissance in the old town. My committee's organised. The carnival entries are pouring in. And the sports day – you've got to enter, all three of you.'

'We've retired, haven't we, Philip?' Emlyn said.

'Nonsense! It'll be fun. The amateur spirit.' He'd finished another pint. 'To the bar!' His face was red and sweaty now. 'It's my treat.'

'Then leave me out,' I said.

But he was up and off to the bar, booming four pints, best bitter.

'Marshall, speak to your father,' Emlyn said. Mash smiled and shrugged his huge shoulders and retired into his own silence. MT returned, slopping beer all over the table, breathing hard. 'How are we doing?' He said, clapping me on the back.

'I'm sinking,' I said.

'Nonsense!' he said and went stamping out to the gents.

'Our night for getting drunk under the table,' Emlyn said. 'Shall we join in?'

'You're on your own, mate' I said.

Emlyn smiled. By the time MT returned he had finished off a glass and was half way down the next.

'My God,' MT said, 'those were the days. Old Tubby Moore, Ted Francis and me – remember me telling you, Marshall?' Mash nodded. 'We had this old Morris. We'd tear up and down the countryside for the women and the pints.' Emlyn winked at me and carried on drinking. 'We were like you – roaring boys! My God, it's a good drop, isn't it? Shall we have some whisky chasers? That's what we had in the old days. Whisky chasers...'

'Not me,' I said hastily. I'd had enough. But Emlyn,

amiable as ever, said whisky chasers would be fine. He wasn't breathing heavily; he wasn't slopping beer all over the place; he wasn't even red in the face.

Half past nine and MT was showing signs of wear, only occasionally coherent. 'You three can be marshalls at the sports day,' he announced at one point, 'then I'll have three marshalls, won't I?' By closing time he was gone, his mouth slack, beer dribbling down his chin and on to his shirt.

Emlyn looked none the worse for wear. 'Better see him home,' he said to Mash, and Mash went to his father's side. 'That's my boy,' MT said. 'Dear old pals, eh? It's been bloody marvellous!' They went lurching across the room, nearly taking the door with them.

'Wait for me outside,' Emlyn said. 'I'm going to be sick.'

'What was that all about?' I asked him as we walked in the soft summer dark.

'Poor old MT. Come to drink us under the table. Well – he's ruined my acid/alkaline balance for sure.'

'You didn't have to take him on.'

He belched. 'No. But it was expected of us. He wanted to show Mash what a boy he can be with a glass in his hand.'

We walked on in silence. 'Maybe he came for Mash – to take him home,' I said. 'Maybe he's heard Mash goes to Lilian's.'

'And that was one way of getting him home? Possible.' He paused by a street lamp and clutched his stomach. 'Oh, dear God, my liver.' Outside the house he said, 'You can come in for drink if you like?' Then he added very quickly, 'and in answer to your query

I haven't been anywhere near Lilian's, so he couldn't have seen me leaving, could he?'

Only a long, wailing siren from one of the waiting ships broke the silence that followed. The night seemed suddenly colder. Questions flitted like bats around us, but we left them unspoken. Emlyn went in. I walked home, all that booze catching up with me now, muttering to myself about sons and fathers. Old MT's blundering, inept intervention. Had they had a man to man talk about Lilian? Oh God! Did MT intend to get plastered with us every night from now on? But it was bad with Mash and MT knew it... I wondered if my old man would have done the same for me, tried to save me. I had my doubts. And I couldn't see Idwal Morton doing it for Emlyn, either.

Sons and fathers. And why were they all such experts on the day before yesterday? 'When I was a boy', they all declared. I couldn't bloody well remember when I was a boy. Well – bits and pieces, of course, when prompted. But not in the way they did.

'What's wrong with you, Roberts?' I said to the lamp post, and the bulb went out. Power had still to be saved for the Country! Belts had to be tightened. Grin and bear it. I leaned against the post. Maybe you had to return yourself to the past, train your memory all over again?

The night gathered around me. The night before Lilian Ridetski's day.

V

On that day, a Saturday, it rained. I spent the morning at home, the afternoon in the Market Hall watching over the shop, while Laura did some sick–visiting. Mash and Emlyn didn't put in an appearance. It was a dull, crawling afternoon, only the occasional customer educating himself in the shop. You could hear Isaac Moss Cobblers whistling some tune as he thumped away at the boots on the far side of the Hall. Trade was slack all round. Mollie Ann Fruits brought me an apple, polishing it on her apron. That German, she said, was a terrible ladies man – did I know? Nell Lewis Crockery had told her, but then Nell and her sister were sex mad. She didn't fancy that German, but some of them couldn't keep their hands off him. Closing her eyes, she said, 'Depravity without wit, is like a toilet without you know what. You enjoy that apple now.'

Laura returned and I escaped to the snooker hall down Maldwyn Street for a while, but I had to promise to be back to lock up because she was going to have her hair done at Lyn Davies' house. At six I moved the stock from the window into the shop and fitted the shutters. I turned the key in the lock and dropped the bunch into my pocket. One of them opened the heavy padlock on the sliding wrought iron gates that were pulled across the entrance to the Hall each night. The last of the shopkeepers to leave – usually Isaac Moss – would see to the gates and make George Garston's property secure. I decided to keep the keys in my pocket. There was a big dance on at the Royal but Ceri wasn't keen on going and the alternative on a wet night in Maelgwyn had to be the other cinema, the Palace. A dry place might well be useful, later.

We had to run from the cinema and were the first couple to reach the porch of the Market Hall. 'Can't stay late,' Ceri whispered. 'My father still thinks I'm twelve.' Other couples were leaping the puddles in our direction. I slipped a key in the padlock and we went into the darkness of the hall, giggling. I remembered to snap the lock incase we became a congregation.

We sat on one of the stalls across from the bookshop, and Ceri proved ready, willing and able – up to a point. When she felt my hand too far up her leg she sat up and said, 'Slow down, Philip Roberts. What a place for that kind of thing.'

'Well come inside the shop, then.' I said eagerly.

'Smells like old socks in there. I bet there's rats.'

She was saying it when we heard the noise.

'What did I tell you?' she added.

We were sitting up, listening. Not rats. A sound as if there were wheels turning, a whirring sound I couldn't put a name to. In the pipes, perhaps. It seemed to come from the far wall of the hall, near where Isaac Moss had his workshop. Suddenly the noise stopped and we were left breathing lightly in a long silence.

Ceri slipped her arm through mine. 'Leave me now and I'll kill you,' and there was a hollow, bumping sound from above, as if something had been knocked over on the top floor of the hall. 'What was that? This isn't good for my nerves.'

She managed a laugh, then we were in silence.

Fright made me noisy. 'That's old George Garston taking an inventory,' I said loudly, my voice making ripples in the darkness.

I lifted her down from the stall and led her over to the bird man's shop and tried the handle. The door was locked. We peered in through the shutters. Just dusty old packing boxes in the corner. 'What are we looking for?' she said.

There wasn't a sound from above. 'Watch this,' I said, and I cupped my hands and yelled through them, 'Hello Georgie!' My voice echoed the length of the hall, caused a rattle in the shutters; appalled me. But there was no response to it from above.

'Home. Now,' Ceri said. 'My nerve's just snapped.'

We ran to the gates, barged through them and the line of snogging couples on the porch. I snapped the padlock shut, disregarded the remarks flung at me, and we hurried through the streets towards Ceri's house.

At her front door she said, 'George Garston – really? What would he be doing up there?'

'Counting his assets.'

'I went out with David Garston. He had this posh accent – after that school he was sent to. Our school wasn't good enough.' We talked for a while, about school. Wasn't Emlyn Morton like a little cherub, remember how he used to organise everybody – usually into trouble? And old Mash. And that woman who taught Biology and used to spit in her hankie every five minutes. Until Ceri's father opened the window above us and said, 'Would you mind resuming the conversation at some other time? It's eleven o'clock!' I kissed her and arranged to meet on the promenade at two, and went home thinking about the Biology teacher, Miss Julius, and how I'd never seen her spit, had I? My forgotten past. I gave no thought to the noises in the Market Hall, but they came back to mind in the morning.

Laura woke me. She was fresh from chapel, her hat still on her head. 'Outside the hall. Maldwyn Street,' she was saying. 'It's terrible. That Mrs Ridetski who keeps the hairdressers. Found her dead this morning, first light. On the pavement. Thrown herself off the hall!'

Police Constable Hughes had found her. It looked as if she had jumped from the roof of the Market Hall. She was wearing a skirt and jumper and a raincoat. Her hair was in curlers. She had been dead for some hours. Liverpool Street knew all the details, but were more curious than sorrowing: Lilian Ridetski wasn't local for a start, and she had a reputation.

'People used to call there,' said Annie Owen who lived next door to us. She looked straight through me.

'If she wanted to do away with herself why didn't she go to the river?' Ned Edwards the postman who lived opposite remarked.

And Laura, speaking to no-one in particular, said, 'Not much charity about this Sunday morning', and closed the door. 'Philip – you knew her didn't you?' I nodded. She made a mess of pouring the boiling water into the teapot. 'Nice woman, was she?'

Soft, fat fingers dealing out the cards. The rippling laugh. Very nice, I said, and we stared at each other until she told me to eat my toast.

I called at Emlyn's house. Down at the boat, Idwal Morton said. 'You'll have heard the news, Philip?'

Idwal was wearing a navy blue suit that shone with age, even a collar and tie, as if he had been out somewhere. 'Dead before she ever hit the ground. They can tell, you know.' His trembling hands gave him a problem as he lit a cigarette. 'Dirty work,' he added. With the sun on him he looked the colour of putty, and there were beads of sweat on his forehead and along his upper lip, although the air was cool. 'It's alleged somebody broke into her shop last night. Living room ransacked.' Velvet cushions piled high on the sofa. 'It's a case of murder certainly. The CID are coming in by the busload.' He made it sound so amusing. 'I wonder what the citizens of this mean city will make of it?'

When I told him I was going he said, 'There will be questions asked – an exposure of intimacies. If you listen carefully you can hear the knocking of knees among the more gregarious of our men about town.'

He never looked at me as he said it. When I reached the corner he was still standing there at the foot of the steps, as if he was uncertain which direction to take.

In a tiny square off the promenade there was a statue of King Edward VII sitting on a throne. Money from the will of an eccentric spinster had placed it there, its blank and baleful eyes staring at the estuary. 'God Save the Prince of Wales', the inscription read at the base, but it was a town joke, target for seagulls and pigeons. There was a big herring gull sitting on the statue's head that Sunday morning. Ceri Price, holding back a small, brown terrier on a lead, was looking up at it.

'I just called at your house,' she said. 'I can't make

it this afternoon. Some of dad's family from the port coming to tea.' She looked at me carefully. 'You do remember we had a date? You look vacant this morning. I've seen a photo of you and Mash and Emlyn Morton sitting up there on King Teddy's lap in form three.' She laughed. 'Down, Tiger!' she told the terrier.

'That noise last night,' I said. 'You know – when we were in the Hall...'

She held her head a little to one side. 'Oh, good God, don't say that! You don't think it was that poor Mrs Ridetski? Is that why you look so absent?' We began walking together, the terrier tangling its lead around our legs. 'But, it couldn't have been her, could it? Poor woman. It wasn't eleven when we left, and they're saying it happened late on. Did you know her?'

Grey eyes looking up at me.

'Yes, I knew her.' A reporter's daughter would know they were crying murder. She knelt to pat the dog's head. I wanted to tell her that there was no way up to the top floor of the Market Hall except through the bird man's shop. She held my arm as she straightened up. I had been one of Lilian's callers. More than anything at that moment I wanted to walk on with her in the sunshine, but we parted at the corner. I had Emlyn to see and questions to ask about Mash.

Emlyn was standing on the black mud under the boat, a can in one hand, a paint brush in the other. 'I've heard,' he said, jabbing the brush into the seam. 'And if Idwal's heard it's murder, then it's murder – so where were you last night?'

'Me?'

He dipped the brush into the can. 'You were about

to ask me where I was last night. More than anything – you were going to ask me where Mash was.' He gave me a swift calculating look. 'We used to visit, didn't we? Stand by for questions. So – where were you?'

'At the pictures.'

'By yourself?'

I was annoyed now. 'Not by myself, no.'

'With Ceri Price, then?' He began to clean his hands with a paraffin rag. 'Good. That clears you.'

'Clears me of what?' I said. There was a heron standing stock still in the river, as if it was listening to us. 'Where the hell were you last night, if it comes to it?'

He held up his hands as if he was holding a trumpet. 'There was a do on. At the Royal. I've got fur on my tongue to prove it!' He poured more paraffin on his hands. 'It was a fantastic session. Me and the band. They were dead until I joined them. I was well and truly on form. Ask around.' He had a familiar, go to hell expression on his face. Then he turned to face me and said quietly, 'Marshall Edmunds got a skinful. I had to walk him home.' He saw the relief on my face, and annoyed me further by saying, 'Mash wouldn't kill poor old bloody Lilian, Philip. Jesus!'

'Oh, for God's sake,' I said. 'But he wasn't so far from killing you, was he?'

He smiled then. 'You have a point there. But he was with me all night. I had him on the drums.' He held both hands to his chest. 'God, I had a pulse beat of a hundred this morning.' We sat on a clean stretch of sand under the dune. 'You saw Idwal then? What did he have to say?'

'Let me tell you about last night,' I said, and I told him about the noise Ceri and I had heard.

'Yes – but what time was she found? And what was she doing out, anyway? And why the Market Hall?'

There was a shout above us on the dune. We got to our feet in time to witness MT come blundering down the dune. 'Ah, boys, there you are,' he cried as he came hurrying towards us. 'I've been looking for you all over. Terrible news! The whole town in a state of shock!' He brushed sand off his trousers. 'This poor woman. We are a peace-loving community, not used to violence.' MT was out of breath. A man in a panic, I thought. 'I suppose Marshall's on board – eh?'

'We haven't seen him,' I said, and he couldn't hide that it was a blow. I turned to Emlyn.

'He'll be sleeping it off,' Emlyn said. 'We over-indulged.'

'Had a skinful, eh?' MT was mopping his forehead. 'You delivered him safe and sound?'

'Well of course I did. Didn't you look in his room?'

MT nodded. 'Must have slipped out of the house early on.' He looked back towards the town. 'His mother – you know what mothers are – running around like an old hen.' He turned and looked hard at the dune. 'Well – I'll stroll back, maybe see him on the way.' But he went charging up the dune and had to pause, winded, at the top. Without a word, Emlyn and I went after him.

VI

Maelgwyn Police Station was a yellow-brick building among old stone houses, off the High Street. It was there we headed after Idwal Morton had met us on the promenade. 'MT,' he'd said, 'It's Marshall. They've got him in the police station.'

Idwal Morton kept up with us all the way and was even able to run up the station steps ahead of us. There he stood, arms out wide, a different man now that he was out of doors, livelier, less contained.

'I advise care and caution, MT,' he said, breathing hard. He had spent a great deal of time in the courts and was fond of legal phrases. 'What is said, is noted down, may be used in evidence...'

'Get out of the way, Idwal,' MT said. 'I can handle this. We are going in for my son, and if we don't get him we'll take this building apart, brick by brick.'

Emlyn looked at me. 'Got your sledgehammer with you, old chap?' A perfect imitation of MT's voice.

'Don't talk like a bloody big boy scout,' Idwal said to MT, and, with a shrug of his thin shoulders, went in ahead of us.

Behind the desk was Sergeant Watts, a long serving member of the force in Maelgwyn. He got to his feet.

'I'm very glad you've come, Mr Edmunds. We've been trying to reach you by telephone.'

'Left off the hook all day Sunday,' MT snapped at him. 'I demand the instant release of my son!'

'Not up to me,' the Sergeant whispered. 'Got higher–ups in. You know how it is.'

'Balls is how it is!' MT roared. I couldn't help smiling. 'I want to see my son now!'

The Sergeant held up one enormous hand, as if to stop all traffic everywhere. 'It so happens,' he said heavily, 'that we are not holding your son.'

'Then release him, Watts. This minute!'

'It so happens that we did not bring your son here.'

'I should think not!'

'It so happens that he came here of his own accord, without pressure of any kind.' The Sergeant was an amateur actor, only too well known in local productions. His pause was nicely timed. 'If you'll excuse me, Mr Edmunds, your son decided he wanted to make a confession.'

MT made a sound as if all the wind had been knocked out of him. 'Confession?' he said. Then he launched himself at the desk. 'Confess to what? I demand as a rate-payer and parent to see him now!'

'It's the higher-ups,' the Sergeant said. 'If you'll sit down, Mr Edmunds, I'll make enquiries for you.' And he stood there, shoulders held back, and waited until we looked as if we were about to join Idwal Morton on the bench before he marched out of the room.

None of us spoke whilst he was out. Emlyn appeared to be reading an old Air Raid Precautions poster on the wall. MT kept on clearing his throat. Idwal Morton stared straight ahead, belching softly every so often. A waiting room tension in the air.

Sergeant Watts was soon back. 'I've arranged it for you, Mr Edmunds,' he said. 'If you'll be so kind as to come this way. It's Chief Inspector Marks, CID.' As he ushered MT out he said to us, 'You are permitted to sit.'

We joined Idwal Morton on the bench under the Air Raid Precautions poster. For most of the time we were silent. Once I began to say something but Idwal said 'Walls have ears,' which earned him a glare from the Sergeant. Idwal kept on going out to the toilet. Emlyn looked around him with interest, as if trying to memorise the place. Half an hour passed.

What happened then happened too quickly for me to remember afterwards. Emlyn nudged me suddenly and said 'OK?' I must have nodded. He got to his feet and marched to the desk, rapped his knuckles on it and said, 'My name is Emlyn Rhys Morton, sane and over twenty one, and I wish to make a confession.'

I saw Sergeant Watts take off his glasses; saw his mouth open. Then Emlyn said, 'And this is Philip Roberts, lately of the army in India, who would like to do the same!'

By then I was standing next to him at the desk, and Idwal Morton was howling behind us, 'Stupid young buggers! You stupid, young buggers.'

Sergeant Watts acted swiftly. He was out of the room in a couple of strides. He left the door wide open and came face to face with a tall man in a grey suit. He said something to the man and jerked a thumb at us.

'Have you taken leave of your senses?' Idwal was yelling at us as the man came to the doorway.

'Both of you?' the man said. He must have used all his clothing coupons on that suit. It was a glove fit, his shirt smooth and starched at the throat, showing at the cuffs crisp and white. But his face was crumpled and tired, pouches under his eyes.

'Don't listen to them!' Idwal roared. 'Playing at silly buggers, that's all!'

'Marks,' the man said, 'Chief Inspector...'

'Morton, E. R., sir,' Emlyn said. 'This is Roberts, P.' You and your pissing brain waves, I thought. 'We also want to confess.'

'Confess to what?' Inspector Marks said. His voice was tired too.

'What about legal representation?' Idwal joined us at the desk. 'What about the caution?'

Inspector Marks sighed. 'You are a parent, obviously. Of one or the other. I am conducting a preliminary enquiry. Nothing more. No one has to say anything if they don't want to. No one has to confess. To anything.' He stared at each of us in turn. 'Is that understood?' I nodded eagerly. 'Then please come this way, quietly and without disturbance of any kind.'

I stepped aside to let Emlyn go first. 'Bloody fascinating, don't you think?' he whispered as he went past. 'I'll bloody fascinate you later,' I told him.

The room was large and bare and smelled of disinfectant. There were two worn tables placed end to end and a number of straight backed chairs. Mash sat in front of the tables. Behind him against the wall sat MT. There was a young, greasy-haired man there as well, across the table from Mash, papers in front of him, an important pencil in his hand. Next to him, his hat tilted back, his gold-rimmed glasses low on his veinous nose, sat Amos Ellyott.

The Inspector spoke, 'I have two more probable confessors, Mr Stubbs.'

Stubbs nodded. 'That makes four, sir.'

'Four?' Idwal Morton cried out. 'How is it four?'

MT stood to attention. 'I have confessed as well,' he announced, and he came over to Emlyn and me and stood between us and clasped our shoulders. 'One for all and all for one – eh, boys?'

Amos Ellyott spoke in a thin, frozen voice, 'You always have the confessors at the beginning, Charles.'

'I know, Mr Ellyott,' the Inspector replied, 'I know!'

'The Chief Constable attended my lectures,' the old man explained. 'The Inspector has most kindly invited me to sit in on this case. As an advisor only, of course.'

The Inspector's face crumpled further. I heard him sigh. 'On such a lovely morning, too,' he muttered.

Poor old Lilian's death a farce already. Mash sat there, head lowered, his huge hands on his lap.

They let me go at seven that evening. Laura said, 'That Emlyn Morton – even when you were a little boy he was always getting you into trouble.' I had been thinking along the same lines all day. 'Your father, if he was alive; just imagine what he'd say! Acting like boys in school. Oh, what a Sunday I've had. Been living on aspirins. And what will the neighbours say? Not that I care what they say, mind. What kind of joke do you call that?' Laura in full force, giving me all I deserved.

But Will Wilkins made a plea for tolerance. 'These young men, Mrs Roberts, they must be given time to settle down.' He always called her Mrs Roberts in my presence. I said I had to have some fresh air and beat a retreat through the back door.

I had been taken to the cottage hospital. I had been stripped and examined, just like in the army. They had taken samples from under my nails. Sent for my demob suit, examined deposits on my shoes. I felt as if I had been rinsed out, then put through the mangle.

And the questions. Inspector Marks doing the asking, Stubbs joining in. Amos Ellyott covering foolscap sheet after foolscap sheet with a scratchy pen, smoking cigarette after cigarette, and occasionally dropping off.

'If you want,' the Inspector said, 'you may talk to me alone.' Amos woke up and said, 'The young man fully understands my position here.' The Inspector gave me a look full of meaning.

They asked me where I had been that Saturday night. Which cinema? What film? Who were the actors? Who had been with me? Who was Ceri Price? (they had already checked with her it was clear). Were we going steady? What time did we leave the cinema and where had we gone? 'The Market Hall?' The Inspector affected surprise. 'It was a wet night,' I explained.

'And you are in the habit of using the Market Hall – for such purpose?' An old puritan face now.

'Sometimes,' I said. Stubbs patted his greasy hair and looked at me with interest. 'On other occasions with Miss Price?' I said no. 'With other young women?' And there I was, labelled town stud. Then came the noises on the top floor. 'Who did you think might be up there?' 'George Garston,' I said. 'And what would he be doing there that time of night?' I couldn't imagine. They asked me a number of questions about Garston. 'You say the shop next door to your father's was locked? Shutters up, empty, I agreed. 'Did you try the door?' In my opinion it was locked. 'But it might have been stuck?' the Inspector said, glancing for approval at Amos Ellyott, but the old man was asleep. It wouldn't open, anyway. 'What exactly did you shout? Describe how you got into the Market Hall. Who else had keys?' It was a thorough going over, but not going anywhere.

That part I could handle easily, but I wasn't so happy with questions about Lilian. How long had I known her? Did I visit her at home? For what purpose? Only to play cards? Had I been intimate with her? How many times? Did she charge for her services?

'She wasn't a pro,' I said. The questions went round a second time, and I wondered at myself because I was able to talk about her as if she had been just a good fuck, and never mind the jokes, the giggles, the deft hands dealing from all over the pack. I still couldn't believe she was dead – my only excuse.

'Not a native of the town, I understand? She was married to a Polish airman who deserted her some five years ago?' I didn't know. 'I see. Did she mention her past life? Most people mention their past, surely?' I had never asked. 'Not at all?' The Inspector's face was slack with disbelief. 'You're hiding something aren't you? And you'd been drinking when you paid your visits? Let me put it like this – was she the kind of person you'd have visited if you had been sober?'

'Of course she was.'

'Really? Aren't you just saying that because the woman's dead?'

'Lilian was very nice...'

'Really?'

'I liked her. I wouldn't have gone to see her if I didn't like her.'

'Really? But only after the pubs and only late at

night when nobody would see you?'

Stubbs looked up at that. He looked at the Inspector. Amos Ellyott did too. He even made a note of it.

'That's how it was,' I said.

'Really?'

'Yes... Really.'

'Someone to satisfy your lust when you were half drunk?' He sounded like the entire temperance movement in session.

'I was totally drunk once or twice.'

'I suppose you learnt tricks like that in the army?'

'Certainly. Which army were you in?'

The Inspector avoided the question. 'Tricks,' he said. A flat, condemning stare. 'Disgusting tricks. A young man of your upbringing, using this woman.' Amos Ellyott was watching him keenly. 'Just an object of lust, wasn't she? Nothing more?'

I had to let him win on that one.

Then we moved to the Market Hall, and I had no answers for him there either. 'Why should she go to the hall? Can you cast any light on that? Assuming that you did talk to her, did she ever mention any connection with the hall? How did she get up there?' Only one way up there, I said. 'So she had a key?' I didn't know who had keys. Some time during the long, waiting day, I had been asking myself these questions. 'Why the roof of the Market Hall?' His questions echoing my thoughts. 'Mrs Ridetski was murdered – do you realise that? Do you realise the full implications of that? Mrs Ridetski was strangled before she was thrown off the roof of the Hall. I want you to think very carefully about that.'

'What d'you think I'm doing?'

And that put me right on the spot. 'In which case, why did you come here today? Why did you say you wanted to make a confession?'

'How did you answer that one, you bloody smart arse?' I asked Emlyn later. 'What the hell were you playing at anyway – pulling a stunt like that?'

'Diversion,' he replied smoothly. 'I told old Marks it was a whim, a fancy, a feeling that we wanted to help old Mash. I apologised.'

'So did I – but he still gave me the biggest bollocking this side of Wales.' We walked on. There was no-one about. No one watching the Police Station for news. Maelgwyn didn't believe in murders. They didn't happen here. And it was Sunday. 'You and your bloody stunts. You always got me in on them, didn't you?'

'I thought you couldn't remember when we were kids?'

I was not to be side-tracked. 'What you did this morning was totally senseless; stupid'.

'Illogical?' He laughed. 'Granted, granted.' We came to the railings on the promenade. The evening mist was coming in off the estuary – a feature of the place after a hot summer's day. Sometimes it became fog that isolated the town from the world. We leaned against the railings and watched its approach.

'You took him home? Right to the door?'

'Right to the door, Philip.'

'I had a feeling this morning that MT had gone up to Mash's room and found a bed that hadn't been slept in...'

'He probably slept on the floor. It was way past two when I got him home. We were plastered, Philip. Gone.'

'And he was in the Royal with you all the time?'

He sighed deeply. 'I've been answering those bloody questions all day. Will you listen? If Mash wanted to knock off poor bloody Lilian he'd have done it in her place – and why should he want to kill her anyway? For God's sake?' The mist had reached the beach. A sudden chill in the air.

'I thought you didn't believe in logic,' I said.

'Tell me what's logical around here. For Mash to confess when he didn't do it? For Marshall Edmunds to know the ins and outs of Market Hall of all places? Is that logic?' I looked down at him. His face was pinched and angry. 'That Inspector, know what he said? Said "Your big friend would appear to be devoid of memory"! So it had to be a piss-taking exercise, hadn't it? Logical in an illogical sort of way?'

He smiled and I had to smile back. 'OK, OK. How long will they keep Mash in?'

'Search me. I'll consult the legal expert when I get home!'

Before we parted on the High Street, he said earnestly, 'I want you to know that I much appreciate your support this morning.'

'My pleasure entirely,' I said.

'But I mean it, Philip...'

'Next time, count me out, OK?' But he was laughing at me, and in time I had to laugh too.

In Liverpool Street there was a house full of silence.

VII

'I am upset all over,' Laura declared. 'Yesterday I lived on drugs and cups of tea. I'm not opening up that shop this morning – I'm not! And this evening you come and lock up for me – all right?' She stared at me keenly across the kitchen table. 'You look washed out to me.'

'It's because I'm worried about what the neighbours will think.'

'You can talk!' She flung at me. 'Smart-mouth talk! They all know you were kept in the police station all day yesterday!' There was a knock on the front door. 'The police!' She cried, clutching at her breasts.

'You go and open it,' I said, 'but don't hurry – it'll give me time to make my getaway.'

'Philip!' She glared at me.

'Sorry, Laura – I'm only joking.'

'It's all joking with you – everything a joke...'

'Yes – well, I'll go and open it, then.'

'You sit there!' She held her arms out wide. 'I'll go!' She backed out of the room. Her nostrils flared when I gave her a little boy wave. I heard the door open – always a sticky one our front door, and I heard MT's booming voice, 'Good morning to you, Laura!' As I went out to the hall I was surprised that I felt relieved.

'Philip!' MT bellowed. 'My dear boy! Laura – I can't

begin to tell you how warm I felt yesterday at a show of camaraderie beyond compare. There we stood – one for all and all for one!'

Laura gave a long, shuddering sigh. Mash appeared behind his father; made our little hallway dark.

'I've brought Marshall along.' MT excelled at the obvious. 'They let my boy go. They let all of us go. And why, you may ask? Because of British justice, Laura. The finest in the world. Not a stain on anybody's character – I was told that in confidence by the Inspector.' MT jiggled coins about in his trouser pocket as he spoke. 'You are not to chastise Laura. You are not to be upset. All you need to be is proud, very proud.'

'Oh, I'm proud all right,' Laura said acidly. I squeezed past her and joined Mash on the pavement. All of Liverpool Street had decided that doorsteps needed a wipe and windows needed a clean.

'Emlyn's gone to look for the car,' Mash said. 'I left it somewhere. You all right, Philip?'

'They're grand these boys, Laura,' MT was saying. 'One for all and all for one...'

'Listen to father,' Mash said, a grin on his face.

His car, Emlyn at the wheel, came roaring down Liverpool Street. 'Get in quick,' Emlyn said, 'the great detective's on his way.' But it was too late. Amos Ellyott came stumping up the street, waving his stick at the curious. It was a warm, sunny morning but he was wearing a long, flapping raincoat and scarf. 'It's obviously going to pour down later,' Emlyn observed. The old man pointed his stick at us. 'If he breaks into a gallop now he'll do us all an injury.'

MT, ever the reception committee, stepped forward. 'Mr Ellyott, this is a great honour.'

'Is it?' The old man hissed.

'It's to Mr Ellyott that thanks are due,' MT, to the whole street. 'His expert guidance and vast experience...'

'Nonsense!' Amos declared. 'Absolute nonsense! No one listened to me. The Chief Inspector, a cretin of some distinction, instructed me to get out. Issued my expulsion! Not even a third rater, that man...'

'They can't see the wood for the trees,' MT said.

'Woods?' Amos snarled. 'Trees? I am not here to discuss flora, my good man! No one is going to push me off the case.' He turned to the three of us. 'I shall require a little assistance from you foolish young men. There is information I need to know.'

'We're going to the boat,' Emlyn said hastily.

'Then I'll come with you.'

MT intervened. 'It may be – how shall I put it – an arduous walk for you, Mr Ellyott.'

'Then they must drive me,' the old man said as he trotted smartly around the car and eased himself on to the passenger seat. He sat there, his chin resting on the handle of his stick, and leered at us.

'Oh, God,' I said.

'Well we can't leave him here,' Emlyn said, 'otherwise your neighbours will complain and you'll be handed a notice to quit.'

Mash drove. Emlyn and I crouched in the back.

'You come and lock up for me,' Laura cried out. 'I'm not staying in that hall with murders going on.'

We had to hump him over the dune, but Amos was suspiciously nimble on the mud and astonished us by climbing unaided up the ladder to the deck.

'Sailing south, eh? I'll come with you. I once

lectured to the police of Hong Kong in Chinese. I also lectured to the police of Samoa in Polynesian. At least I think it was Polynesian. I am a linguist of some repute.'

'Oh, I bet,' Emlyn said as we settled him down on a deck chair.

'Mine was a brilliant family. My father was an antiquarian and a diarist. If one wants to make water what does one do? Over the side?'

'Just mind which way the wind's blowing,' Emlyn said as we began to sort out the painting gear.

Mash suddenly got to his feet and announced very simply, 'I'm sorry Lilian's dead – that's all.' We all were, Emlyn assured him. Mash nodded firmly, then he picked up a can and a couple of brushes and began to hum as he stepped on to the ladder and climbed down.

'So,' the old man said softly, 'so.'

'Write it down in your notebook,' Emlyn said, 'but it wasn't Mash – for sure.'

'And that's why you decided to confess, both of you? To point out how absurd it was to hold your friend?' Amos tilted his hat over his eyes. 'Dear me! How noble of you. Or was it because you knew the authorities were bound to get round to you three in time?' Up came the brim of his hat. He stared at us keenly over his glasses. 'And they will return to you. The relief is only temporary. Once they've interviewed other gentlemen callers. Once they've checked your stories.'

'It's possible you may never leave this ship alive,' Emlyn said. 'Grab a paintbrush or go to sleep.'

Amos Ellyott cackled like an old hen. 'The confessors! What an incredible notion. Straight out of *Boys' Own*, my worldly friends...'

'How did Mash go on with them?' Emlyn enquired.

'I am not prepared to divulge information of that kind,' Amos replied stiffly. 'Not to suspects.'

'In which case,' Emlyn said, 'may every passing seagull shit on you!'

Amos chuckled, his chin now deep in his scarf. 'But what about a man burnt to death in pound notes? Incinerated in genuine notes of the realm, my absurd friends? Now there's a notion for you.' And he left us hanging on that, and slept.

We patched and caulked and painted. Mash sang for most of the afternoon. The old river stank. We were on an island, cut off from the town. We had work to do, and work cancelled out thinking; served as a temporary cure for shock.

Once during the afternoon Emlyn came up the ladder to say he had decided that we had to do a turn for the carnival. 'We're going to be a jazz band on a lorry and to hell with them,' he said. 'All we need is a white shirt and a bow tie.' I told him to piss off. No more stunts for me. Especially now. 'Oh God,' he said, 'was yesterday too much for you? I'm sorry. But we can't let old MT down.' Piss off, I said. 'We can't, Philip. We've promised.' You did the promising. 'Yes but you'll think it over, won't you? Give it some thought?' Today I'm not doing any thinking – about anything. 'Oh well, – tomorrow, then. We'll have a chat about it tomorrow.'

I was alone with Amos when he woke up. 'She was killed inside the Market Hall,' he said. 'Did you know?'

'Just tell me how she got up there,' I said. 'That door was locked, and where would she get the keys, tell me? She'd need a key for the padlock on the gates too.'

'So you have been thinking. And you don't know there is another way up there? Oh come now – you must know. Good God, everybody else in the Market Hall knows. Didn't you ask your stepmother?'

He was sitting up now, giving me all his attention. 'We had other things to talk about,' I said. 'Well go on.'

'A lift,' he said. 'At the far end of the Hall. Surely you remember that from your boyhood?'

'That old thing? You pulled yourself up with a rope? Well of course I remember it. They were going to have film shows up there. Before the war. It was to carry all the equipment up. They did away with it.'

Amos preened his moustache. 'Perhaps I had better come with you to lock up the shop for Mrs Roberts.'

On the way back Mash ran over a nail and we had to get the spare wheel out. Amos Ellyott took my arm.

'Philip and I can't wait,' he said to Emlyn. 'We must reach the lady in the shop before the assassin strikes again.' He pointed his stick up the High Street and Emlyn shouted 'Charge!' And the old man chuckled deep in his throat as we set off.

'Don't let go of my arm,' he warned me, 'but contrive to keep your distance at the same item. My bones are very brittle.' People stopped to stare at us. Ceri Price thought we looked a treat. She even came over to tell us. 'I was married to a lovely girl like that,' Amos declared loudly outside Woolworth's. 'She left me, of course.'

Laura was struggling with the shutters when we arrived and was only too pleased to let me finish the job. 'There is no danger, Madam,' Amos called after her, but that only made her heels click a little bit faster on the stone floor of the Hall. I had expected a policeman on guard but there was none. All the shops were shut except for Isaac Moss Cobblers. Amos took a small length of wire from his pocket and slipped it into the lock of the bird man's shop. There was a click.

'Follow me,' he ordered as he went in. 'I take full responsibility. Don't be afraid.' I brushed past him and took the stairs two at a time. I was looking down the aisle of chairs when he came panting up. The screen that had been painted on the wall had a door in it now, and it was open. In one corner there was an open stairway to the roof.

'Observe dimensions,' Amos said. 'Surely you must have noticed the discrepancy in dimensions when you came here before?'

'I wasn't looking for discrepancies,' I replied as I went on ahead of him to the door. Through it there was another room, wide as the hall, I guessed. A black room without windows. Amos all but pushed me in. He produced a small torch and let the beam roam along the walls. Totally empty and very clean.

'Mr George Garston has reported the loss of a bunch of keys,' Amos said. 'Interesting, don't you think?' The beam of the torch was fixed on a second, narrower stairway leading to the roof. 'Intriguing, intriguing. An empty room. A suspiciously clean and empty room, wouldn't you say? And dimensions – think about dimensions here too.' A circle of light fingering the room. 'It was here she came. It was here she was killed.'

We stood on the open roof and looked down at the chimneys of the old town. I was glad to be up there, even if heights weren't for me.

'Down there – Maldwyn Street,' Amos said. 'Her

body was cast forth from here, wouldn't you say?'

As he said it Mash and Emlyn came up the stairs into the cabin-like structure on the roof. Following them closely came the Inspector's assistant, Mr Stubbs, who was protesting, 'Not allowed! You have no right to be here! This is evidence!' He banged his head as he came through the narrow doorway on to the roof and stood there patting his gleaming hair. 'Mr Ellyott! Please! With all due respect!'

But we were watching Mash. He had gone directly to the side that overlooked Maldwyn Street and was looking down, swaying there. 'Hey – fire escape!' He called to us over his shoulder. Then he went closer to the edge and began to wave his arms about, his knees bending. Emlyn and I ran for him. I grabbed the back of his trousers. He fell on top of us and I could hear his laughter roaring in my ears. 'Wasn't going to jump!' he protested. 'Just showing the fire escape, that's all!'

'You made me very ill,' Emlyn told him.

'If you please, Mr Ellyott,' Stubbs called out despairingly. 'I don't want to have to report you.' Emlyn, Mash and I went, meek as schoolboys, but Amos held on for a while to give Mr Stubbs some advice about Police methods in an efficient force.

But we were all in the empty room when we heard the sound of wheels turning, smoothly, softly, turning in oil. A sound, I reasoned, that you could hear only in the quiet of night. It seemed to come from the ground floor – about where Isaac Moss Cobblers had his shop, I thought. And it was rising to our level, like wheels turning in the wall.

'There will be a door,' Amos whispered, his torch searching. 'A door that can only be opened from inside the lift.' Out of the floor the noise came. It ended with a snap. Then there was silence.

The beam from Amos's torch was steady on one spot. The wall came away as a small door opened and we were looking at Inspector Marks' backside as he eased himself out. He turned to face us. A hand came up to hold back the glare from the torch. 'Mr Ellyott,' he said, 'is it your intention to blind me?'

'You have no right whatsoever to be on these premises,' the Inspector said. Amos flashing his torch into the lift. Amos inside the lift. 'Mr Ellyott, please! I don't want to impose sanctions!' Amos pulled the door shut. We heard the lift descend. 'I am ordering you all to keep out of this,' Marks thundered. 'Especially that old man!'

'Inspector,' came Emlyn's voice out of the darkness, 'what if he has a heart attack in there?'

Marks' torch came on, a powerful beam that burnt on the narrow door. 'Heart attack?' He said, 'Oh my God, no!' The lift came to a halt; Amos was having some trouble with the door. 'Are you all right Mr Ellyott? It's a catch on the right hand side.'

The door swung open and Amos emerged. 'Mr Garston took some time to tell you about this contraption, didn't he Marks?' The Inspector was brushing dust off the old man's shoulder. 'Will you stop patting me, man?'

'You know the rules, Mr Ellyott. There can be no discussion. None whatsoever...'

'Down there,' Amos said, 'what is there down there?' I remembered then. 'A loading bay of some kind?'

'A garage,' the Inspector said. 'Now... Come on.'

'Belonging to Garston?' A large lean-to structure

in that most vile of building materials – corrugated iron. Have you charged him yet?'

The Inspector's torch was pointing at the ceiling. I saw him draw himself up to his full height, saw him adjust a cuff, straighten his tie. 'Mr Ellyott – you ought to know better than to ask. Besides, is it a crime to possess a garage? Is it a crime to possess a lift?'

'It is to withhold evidence,' Amos snapped, and they had a quick slanging match which Emlyn broke up by asking if it was all right to have a ride in the lift.

'How long was it before he told you there was a lift?' Amos persisted.

'That will do!' the Inspector roared. 'I now order you to leave these premises. All of you! At once!'

Amos waved his torch at us as he came stumping after us down the aisle between the chairs. 'I have friends in high places,' he was muttering. 'I am not to be spoken to in that tone of voice.' But out in the street his mood changed. 'Now it becomes fascinating,' he said. 'Mr George Garston – isn't he a card? Only answers the question. Volunteers nothing. I took it upon myself to survey these outbuildings, you know. Special lock, would you believe? And expensive. Mr Garston had something to hide. We must draw him out – like a boil.'

We went out on the town that evening, and I thought it was all very embarrassing because, wherever we went, the conversation took a dive and was some time rising again. 'Notorious at last,' Emlyn said with satisfaction.

The only dance was in the Girl Guide Hut in the sand hills on the way to the golf club. Music courtesy of gramophone record. The dance was due to finish at eleven. We arrived at twenty to, the wrong place, and the wrong time, and I was about to suggest a retreat until I saw Ceri was there. MT Edmunds was building up to the climax of his speech at that point.

'Let us build our town into the premier resort on this lovely coast,' he declaimed. 'Big ends have small beginnings!' I saw Ceri raise a hand to hide a smile. She was standing next to Mrs Williams-Brown who was famous for being in charge of the Brownies and who was fat and hearty and didn't like our appearance one little bit. 'You young people,' said MT, one of his posters on display, 'you are the flowers of our town. Support must come from you.' He waved his poster like a banner. 'Turn up in your hundreds. Join in. Revive our beautiful town!' Mrs Williams-Brown boomed out a 'hear, hear!' And without ceremony brought the speech to an end with the next record at full volume. Even so, MT managed the last word, 'On with the dance,' he cried, 'let joy be unconfined!' Then he swept out, pausing only to give the three of us a friendly punch, the dedicated man himself, and to hell with murder and apathy and a poor weather forecast.

'You owe me a dance,' Ceri said. 'My word, you smell like a brewery.'

'Get your coat – I'll walk you home.'

But she insisted on a dance. 'I came to give old Williams-Brown a hand with the kids,' she said, 'until their mothers come to collect. Don't stand so stiff, for goodness' sake. It's like dancing with a lamp post.'

Mash and Emlyn were being daft and dancing with two little girls. 'Isn't Emlyn Morton a cherub,' Ceri said as the last waltz began. 'I remember dancing with him before the war. He dared me to climb the flagpole and I took him on.' Then we stopped dancing and stood still in the middle of the floor and watched two mothers in macs and scarves grab their children away from Emlyn and Mash. Emlyn was tight-lipped; Mash bewildered.

They came over to us. 'We're off,' Emlyn said. 'See you're fixed up, Philip.' We watched them go, a platoon of mothers at the door stepping aside for them.

Ceri said grimly, 'You stand there where everyone can see you. I'll get my coat.'

We walked slowly along the narrow road through the sand hills. 'They're not going to make public enemies of my friends,' she said. 'You should have heard what my father said when the police came to see me.' I told her about the station and the visit to the Market Hall, and Amos Ellyott. 'Now him,' she said, 'he drops in on us – for hours! But you and Emlyn Morton and Mash have got the tongues wagging – you know that, don't you?'

'Bound to,' I said.

'She was a nice woman. Bit of a hard case. It was a scream when you went there to have your hair done – the things she came out with.' She squeezed my arm. 'Did you like her?'

Lilian Ridetski, fat fingers caressing the cards. Her death hit me then. 'Of course I liked her.'

She drew me to a halt and reached up and kissed me on the cheek. 'I'm glad you said that.'

'We all liked her.'

'And that.' I held on to her then, and she was warm and encouraging until I pushed her back against a gorse bush. 'Ow! My bum! God – the places you take me!' She was saying that when we heard a shout ahead.

We ran forward. Out of the darkness MT came staggering, a handkerchief to his face. 'Oh my goodness,' he said through it, 'what a terrible nosebleed.'

Then I heard a car door slam shut. Its lights came on as it moved off using too many revs. MT was breathing heavily, 'Thank God it's you Philip.' Not a nosebleed, I decided. MT had just been thumped.

'What's going on, Mr Edmunds? Whose car was that?'

'Now Philip – young lady, know your father well of course – I implore you. On your word of honour say nothing about this to anyone, please. Please.' He touched his nose, the handkerchief white in the darkness. 'It's the embarrassment, you see.'

I had a clean handkerchief and I gave it to him. He made a speech of thanks and found more ways to apologise than I thought possible. He walked away after wishing us half a dozen good nights, but called me over before he finally went to whisper urgently. 'Not a word of this to Marshall – will you promise on your honour?' I said of course. 'And the young lady?'

'She'll keep quiet too,' I assured him.

'What have I got to keep quiet about?' Ceri enquired as we walked on.

'Doesn't want anybody to know he's been in a fight.'

'Oh – do you suppose George Garston's anti sports and carnival like the rest of the town?'

'Why George Garston?'

'His car,' she said. 'I'm positive. And do you know the police have been talking to David Garston too?' She laughed softly. 'When your old man's a gentleman of the press you hear it all.'

VIII

During the war, Maelgwyn's population had taken a leap. Out of the cities had come the refugees from the bombs, most of them elderly, most of them well–heeled. One of the features of the town was the number of women you saw trotting around to the shops, chattering over cups of tea, taking the air on the promenade. Little, birdlike women in floral dresses and ancient hats, monied widows and spinster ladies, firm believers in keeping themselves to themselves who had decided not to return to the big towns when peace finally arrived. Such a one was Catherine Jane Porterhouse, who was discovered at ten on that Tuesday morning, perched on King Teddy's lap. Dead of strangulation.

'It's a maniac loose,' Laura declared. 'That old statue – just imagine – she was sitting on his knee, flowers in her hand. Wild flowers. She collected them. At night.'

'At night?'

'They say she might have been there for days. Nobody ever looks at that old statue anyway. High old time the council pulled it down.'

'There was nobody on his knee on Sunday morning,' I said.

The remark silenced her. She stared at me keenly. 'You won't have to go to the police station because of her, will you?' She had hurried back from the shop with the news, her working hat still on her head. Now her cheeks flushed to the same colour – pink. 'You know what I mean, don't you? Don't know if I'm coming or going, I don't. It's a maniac loose. We never had that – not even when the troops were here.'

'Did you know her? Mrs Porterhouse?'

'Miss,' she said with a shake of the head. 'Mollie Ann says she's seen her, but nobody seems to know anything about her. She was renting some rooms – that place near the Royal on the front. George Garston's, they say – got property everywhere that man. She came from a very good family Yorkshire way. Wool, Mollie Ann says. But nobody really knows much about her. Know what they're like, don't you? Don't mix. Just come here to live by themselves and mind their own business. It's terrible, isn't it? Don't you think it's terrible?'

'You're having me on.'

'It's true, Philip.'

'She picked wild flowers at night?'

'She was strangled – like – you know.' Laura sitting down now, settling down too. She had rushed back to tell me. I wondered what she had expected to find. An empty house? The police at the door.

'King Teddy's lap? Honestly?'

Now she was embarrassed. 'I was just like you. Couldn't believe it, neither.' Sweat shone on her forehead. 'I thought I'd let you know.' She fanned herself with the *Daily Mirror*. 'Goodness – isn't it hot? It's a heat wave on the way, they say. Even hot in the Market Hall.' A suspect, that's what I was.

‘Who found her?’

She gulped. ‘Marshall Edmunds. He was running or something and he happened to look up – and he saw her. Reported it to the police.’

‘It’s a fact,’ Emlyn said. ‘It would have to be old Mash, wouldn’t it? He was training, would you believe? Pounding up the prom and he spots this old girl up there. Just goes to show – if you want to hide something then leave it in a prominent place.’

We were aboard the *Ariadne*, sitting on some sackcloth because the roof of the cabin was so hot. Mash was giving another coat of red paint to the old boat’s keel. He’d looked up and she was sitting there on the old King’s knee, sea holly in her hand. He was very proud that he had been the one to find her, Emlyn said. But they held him at the police station all morning.

Emlyn pointed towards the dune ‘Oh God, look what’s coming – anyone for tennis? You can smell the mothballs from here!’

Amos Ellyott stood on top of the dune, his stick raised like a sword. He was wearing a white shirt with billowing sleeves, a tie and white cricket flannels of stunning tightness. On his head the biggest straw hat. ‘Halloo there,’ he called, ‘it is I, Ellyott!’

I suggested that we hide, but Emlyn went down to escort him over the mud and heave him, rung by rung, up the ladder. And all of that afternoon under a burning sun the old man talked death from the deck chair. He knew little more than we did about Miss Porterhouse, but he was positive that she had died of strangulation. He found that fascinating. The same method as before. Some sort of strap had been used.

Bizarre, the old man said, bizarre and puzzling. No one, as yet, had come forward to claim her, either.

'No one's claimed Lilian – is that what you mean?' I said.

Two ladies of such different backgrounds, he went on. Lilian Ridetski had no relations because of an accident of birth; Miss Porterhouse would probably have outlived hers – and she had never been married to a Polish airman, now officially listed as a deserter. Andrei Ridetski. A very fastidious gentleman. Something of a dandy, and rumoured to be involved in the underworld of Warsaw.

Had he perhaps taken flight because of the lady's sexual appetite? 'That is a possibility, my friends – but I doubt such a reason would instigate him opting for desertion in a foreign land, for leaving a prospering little business, and a warm little nest. The premises were in the lady's name, but they were purchased by Ridetski, who, we are led to believe is a penniless Polish refugee. Where did the money come from? Was there, perhaps, assistance? There are claims that he has been sighted, he added from behind a white handkerchief which now covered his face.

'Seen here – in Maelgwyn?' I asked.

'Elsewhere,' Amos replied. 'Persons answering to his description.'

Later he awoke to tell us that George Garston had admitted finally that he had made use of the secret room on the top floor to store unspecified goods.

'George Garston would be involved in the black market, wouldn't you say? But on the night in question he was attending a concert in the village hall at Brynberth. He was accompanied by his son, he claims. It was an affair that continued well into the night. But there would have been time. There is always time when one is desperate.' He appeared to have gone to sleep again. We stretched out and surrendered to the heat.

'However,' he said. We both sat up. Beneath us we could hear the old boat's timbers shrinking, 'let us consider some other intriguing factors...'

'Not the day for considering anything,' Emlyn protested. 'I think I've got heat stroke.'

Amos Ellyott's thin, precise voice, rasped on relentlessly. 'Mrs Ridetski was a lady who loved finery – a gaudy dresser, I am given to understand. Yet, on the night in question, she had not dressed in her usual fashion. We must therefore assume that the summons had been urgent, unexpected and important. Summoned by a familiar, I am led to conclude.' He gave us a long silent spell to ensure that we thought about it. 'Well – what d'you say?'

'If you say so,' Emlyn said. 'I mean – yes.' He appealed to me. 'You take over – the heat's got me.'

'Nonsense,' Amos said. 'You are simply refusing to think. Mrs Ridetski had a key. She went in answer to a summons. The same key opened the garage door as well as the door to the lift contraption. She ascended.' His mottled hands came up and pulled at an imaginary rope. 'And there was someone waiting, someone who she had hurried to, confidently. Tell me – why have you not confessed to the murder of Miss Porterhouse?'

'I beg your pardon?' Emlyn said.

'The Inspector will want to know. He will send for you before the day is out. The three of you. Marshall's parent too. All the confessors. He will want to know why you made a special case of Lilian Ridetski. I trust you have your answers and your alibis?'

'Well, bugger me,' Emlyn said lightly. 'I should throw you off my ship. We're suspects, are we?'

'Only because you have invited suspicion, you foolish, naive young men,' Amos said before he went to sleep once more.

At five that evening I was interviewed by Inspector Marks. At six, Emlyn. At seven Mash, and they kept him in for a long time. They had to throw MT out of the police station.

'OK,' Emlyn said, 'I know I'm to blame – but you don't really care what they think in this shitty little town, do you?'

'It isn't that,' I said.

'Well – you never used to care. You didn't give a fuck for anybody. You were famous for it.'

'Me? Famous? When?'

'At school. Ask anybody.' We had given Mash an escort home and we were standing outside Emlyn's house in the Crescent. Some women in the King's Arms had actually pointed the finger at us. 'Now look – what we'll have to do is get this bugger caught. I mean, I'm like you. I don't give a sod what the bloody town thinks. But what we'll do is we'll set a trap. He's local all right and he's gone off his nut, so once and for all, to stop all this harassing we're getting because I made a bit of a balls of it, we'll catch him, preferably in the act!' He was facing me, standing on his toes, he eyes shining.

'Good night,' I said. 'You go to your bo–bo's and read a comic. Count me out.' I walked away from him.

'Philip,' he called after me.

'Bollocks,' I called back.

That night Lilian's shop was burgled. Nothing was taken, nothing much disturbed, except that someone stripped a length of wallpaper off one of the walls in Lilian's bedroom. 'Something there behind a picture on the wall,' Laura said, her eyes quick and wide. 'Fancy!'

'It'll be an envelope,' Emlyn told her with great assurance. 'Brown manila. With plans for an atomic bomb!'

'Good heavens!' Laura said, 'how d'you know?' Then she laughed. 'You're joking. Having me on.'

Laura, perched on a stool outside the shop, swung out with her rolled up *Daily Mirror* and caught him across the ear. 'Get away,' she said, 'clear off the both of you!' Only be back to close the shop for her in case the maniac was lying in wait behind the bookshelves.

'Leave it open,' I suggested. 'Maybe he'll pinch the stock.'

'I should be so lucky,' she shouted after us.

We wandered around the hall. 'Isn't this great?' Emlyn said. 'Messing about – just like when we were kids on those long summer holidays. I remember going up and down like a yo–yo in that old lift – but I thought they'd done away with it too.'

'Second time someone's broken into Lilian's place,' I said. 'Maybe old man Ridetski's come home.'

'Could be,' he agreed, 'but why pick on Miss Porterhouse?' He said it to Mollie Ann Fruits, and she, in a voice that came from deep inside said, 'It's only the beginning – mark my words!'

Outside in the sunshine Emlyn said, 'We are going

to give MT a lift? The Jazz Band.'

'Without me,' I said promptly.

'I want us all in whites. Black bow tie. Dark specs. The wagon's fixed. Mash on drums. Sid Bates'll be on piano – I've fixed that as well. You on banjo.'

'Look, I've no strings on the fucking banjo,' I said.

'All the fucking better for that,' he went on smoothly. 'I knew I could rely on you!'

MT's carnival and sports day were fixed for the Friday, and in spite of forecasts of depressions on the way, the days leading up to it blazed, each one hotter than the last.

'Oh – this old heat wave,' Laura complained, 'makes all them books sweat in the shop.' But the whole town came out to rejoice in it, fan itself, and take the air and crowd the pubs. Talk of murders and inquests and funerals went by the board. Heat and sunshine's deaths and dying antidote.

I took Ceri out each day and to hell with working on the boat. The town council had officially boycotted the carnival and sports day, she told me. They had even tried, and failed, to secure a police ban on the procession because of the grave happenings in the town. The heat and the sunshine had met a barrier at the walls of the Council Chamber. To hell with grave happenings too, I thought. There was Ceri running out of the sea, Ceri smiling in the sun, Ceri's voice in my head. I would have to work on keeping her away from David Garston who was sniffing around. It was she who told me that David had failed his exams. It was Amos Ellyott who told me that the police interviewed David every day, and were not happy with his story.

But that wasn't why Mash thumped him in the saloon bar of the King's Arms. No one knew why he did it. David walked in. Mash threw a punch at him. And afterwards he couldn't remember doing it.

The depression arrived the morning of MT's carnival. A boisterous wind sprang up from the estuary with havoc in mind, a startling dip in temperature, grey clouds obscuring the sun. It made the parade that was assembling in the yard of the Royal Hotel look even thinner that it was.

'Only three entries in the decorated bicycle class,' MT said, 'but never mind, never mind. It will look fine once we string along.' He had decided to stick to the original route in spite of warnings about the wind on the promenade. The newer part of town first, then the old, up to the High Street and back to the Royal. 'Look at the children,' he cried out. 'Aren't they marvellous?'

There were four shivering fairies, one with a broken wand; two little girls in Welsh costume who kept chasing their hats and three little boys dressed as ghosts. Numerous soldiers with sooty faces, twenty or more of whom it was difficult to say exactly what they were, and a little girl named Sian Thomas, not in fancy dress at all, who said she was the atomic bomb. Among the adults were John James as Mae West. Emlyn could remember him as Mae West in 1935, and at every subsequent carnival.

'A noble effort all round,' MT declared. 'Now – into line everybody.'

Only three floats had assembled, two of them horse drawn because of the petrol rationing. On one of these were the Women's Institute as 'The Merry Wives of Windsor', crinolines billowing, wigs, and flower baskets. The other was a small cart covered with flowers, a highly professional job, a trade entry from a new shop in the High Street – 'Bilton's for Better Blooms' in gold lettering on either side of the mound of blossoms, a small pot pixie rising above them all. We followed this on one of MT's lorries. The Jazz Band. Emlyn was already warming up. Mash banging enthusiastically on the drums, Sid Bates trying to unstick the keys on the old upright that Emlyn had borrowed, and me with my banjo wishing it was all over. Amos Ellyott sat at the rear of the lorry on an ancient cane chair. 'If anybody asks,' Emlyn said, 'tell them he's the singer.' MT wouldn't give us a prize because that would have been favouritism.

He headed the procession, in front of the Brynbach Silver Band. He was wearing a black jacket, pinstriped trousers, a bowler on his head. And he carried a rolled umbrella, and made of it a drum-major's stick. He blew his whistle. The Band struck up. We moved off. Very few came to watch us in the new part of town, but faces at windows peered at us. Emlyn gestured at them with his trumpet and curtains fell back into place.

'It's a cold audience,' he observed. 'When that bloody band stops murdering all the men of Harlech, we'll give them "I Got Rhythm," OK? After four.'

Our turn to murder, as we turned the corner on to the promenade.

It was deserted, ravaged by the wind. The procession leaned against it, broke up to retrieve hats and flowers and strips of tissue paper and the Brynbach Silver Band ran out of puff. Now we were straggled. Blossoms from 'Bilton's for Better Blooms' took to the air. The promenade went on for as long as the Sahara Desert.

'Everybody squat down,' Emlyn ordered. 'We'll hit 'em for six in town.'

And there the band revived, but now the procession was bruised. Miss Lottie Hughes retired, chilled. But Mae West marched on, and so did the children. There was a state of emergency aboard 'The Merry Wives of Windsor', and one side of the flower cart read 'Bil or etter looms'.

'Keep it up, you chaps,' MT told us, and went bounding to take his place at the front.

But it was worse in the town. There the wind came at us suddenly around corners, and in a more confined space had greater force. It slashed and punched, caught the procession suddenly and unaware, guard down. As we entered the High Street I saw Laura standing with Will Wilkins outside his shop.

'Oh, what a shame,' she cried, 'don't get pneumonia, will you?' I saw Ceri too, and her hand came up to her mouth and she bit on a knuckle – a familiar gesture – to hide a smile. Then, twenty yards or so down the High Street, where the watchers were two deep on the pavement, we stalled.

I stuck my head inside the cab. The driver was making no effort to re-start. 'Don't tell me we have to push this bloody wagon,' I said. He turned and looked up at me, bloodshot eyes rolling. 'Bloody hell, man! Thought I saw a hand come up then! In the middle of them flowers! On that bloody cart!'

I banged my head and heard myself tell him to get on with it, for God's sake, everybody laughing their heads off at us. He re-started the cab and we set off with such a jerk that the piano nearly fell on Sid Bates.

'He says he saw a hand come up,' I said to Emlyn, and he said, 'Jack's been at the bottle for years.' But he came to my side and we rested our elbows on the roof of the cab and stared ahead. Sid Bates stopped thumping on the piano. Amos Ellyott stumbled over to join us. Only Mash kept at it, brushes in his hands, his foot steady on the bass pedal.

We drew closer to the cart. And she was there, an arm exposed, a shoe pointing at the sky, couched among 'Bilton's for Better Blooms'. The drum went swish, swish, thump, swish, swish. Someone at an open window above a shop cried out. We stalled again. The driver yanked the hand brake up and switched off the ignition. He heaved the door open and nearly fell out. He slammed the door shut. 'That's me – finished,' he said, 'nobody told me it was a fucking funeral!' And off he went, abandoned us, and we stood and watched the cart's slow progress all the way down the High Street. And it was deathly quiet, except for Mash going swish, swish, thump, swish, swish on the drums.

IX

'A spinster lady, name of Sweeney,' Amos Ellyott explained yet again. 'Amy Gertrude Sweeney, daughter of a fruit importer, lately of Southampton, of independent means, like Miss Porterhouse, and of eccentric habits, again like that poor lady. Miss Sweeney believed in sea water applied to the feet at night, as a medical aid.'

A paddle in the dark and someone waiting. I looked across the promenade at the estuary, the tide out, the big ships motionless in the channel, white evening clouds banked low and suppressed a shiver.

'Unlike Miss Porterhouse, Miss Sweeney was quite well known. She was given to lecturing on a matter of some concern to those people who have sought sanctuary here – health.'

Ever since the carnival the comments of the town had echoed the old man's. Not as precise perhaps but in the same vein – all wonder and irony, with sorrow and compassion only afterthoughts. Miss Sweeney dead had put in a public appearance, after all. 'Did you see her?' was the question. The town was getting used to murders. A kind of relish in the way they spoke.

'There is no immediate link between Mrs Ridetski, Miss Porterhouse and Miss Sweeney, although it is not beyond the bounds of possibility that the two spinster ladies may well have utilised the services of Mrs Ridetski. They were not called to the Market Hall, but I am assured that the method of despatch was the same.' He decided then that he was exhausted and headed for one of the benches on the promenade. 'The style is everything, is it not?' He went on. 'Your interviews with that idiot were brief, I understand?'

'We didn't do this one,' Emlyn said.

'But Marshall was detained for some considerable time, was he not?'

'Only because it takes him longer to tell them he didn't do it.'

Amos nodded. 'Bilton's flower cart, finishing touches apart, was made up late last evening, and left in the yard of the Royal under a tarpaulin. Miss Sweeney lived in a bungalow no more than twenty yards from the Royal. Fairhaven, she called it, a port she failed to make.'

'It's all so bloody amusing,' I remarked to no one in particular.

'Oh, beyond joking,' the old man agreed as he tried to stand. 'A surfeit of victims, I agree.' His joints had locked and we had to go through the business of straightening him. We were on our way to the Grange in response to an urgent message from Mrs Edmunds. It was to do with Mash, I knew, and I was anxious to get there, impatient with the old man who was giggling at our touch. 'The press are here,' he said as we resumed our walk. 'The town has been mentioned on the wireless. Infamy fascinates. I think the police force of the entire country is in attendance. Poor Inspector Marks.'

As we came up to the Grange he was saying, 'I am intrigued by an emerging pattern. Our assassin does not rob, indulges in no sexual malpractice...'

'Do you mind?' Emlyn said. 'You're making me feel ill – for God's sake Philip, knock on the damn door.'

I rattled the brass knocker.

'Our assassin would appear to be incapable of leaving his victims alone.' Amos droned on. 'I should say his or her victims, of course.' And the door opened, and Sylvia Edmunds stood there asking us to come in.

She sat in a high-backed wickerwork chair and she knitted, and the click of the needles punctuated the conversation. Hands big as a man's jabbing at a pattern, eyes concealed behind the thick lenses of her glasses. A driven woman, I felt. And she came straight to the point. How long is this to go on for? How many more times were they going to drag Marshall in for questioning? Had they asked us questions? Did they want to know where we were last night?

'In the bath, that's what I told them,' Emlyn said. 'And that's where I was – after I brought Mash home.'

'Marshall,' she corrected him. 'Marshall. That absurd name you give him...'

'I've no alibi.' I told them.

'Marshall was here with me until he went to bed, and I went up to see him afterwards. Why can't they leave him alone? They're picking on him.' She spoke to Emlyn most of the time. 'You've seen terrible things. You've been in the hands of the enemy. You know what questions are like.' Her voice reasonable, all her anger in the needles. 'Do you know where they are now? Him and Marshall? Cutting grass! Marking out the park for his sports day! After that dreadful, dreadful farce this afternoon. What a response – the sports day cancelled, until tomorrow!' Her feet were big, her legs sinewy. Dark fuzz of hair along her arms. 'There are things I need to know. Why did Marshall hit David Garston, Philip?'

The question caught me off guard. I had been quite prepared to let Emlyn do the talking.

'Maybe he'd had a bit too much to drink,' Emlyn broke in.

'Does he get violent with drink, then?' The question was addressed to me.

'Not usually. He doesn't usually...'

'He didn't have any drink in him when he attacked Emlyn, did he? Well – come on. Don't be evasive, Philip. Your father was always evasive...'

'Not a question of being evasive.'

'Facts, then. You were there. What would have happened to Emlyn had you not been there? What started it off? Come on – tell me.'

Emlyn came to my rescue. 'Philip was up on deck. It wasn't an attack really. We were just fooling about, ragging each other – and it got out of hand.' He was smiling there, a tanned, open face, a con man to his fingertips. 'When you're ragging about things get serious. Maybe I stood on his toes, or something. Mash – Marshall's got dead-sensitive toes.' He grinned at her, but she was not amused.

'You're his best friend,' she said. 'Even when you were small. He wouldn't attack you, would he?'

'There wasn't an attack – as such.'

She paused in her knitting to adjust her spectacles. 'Well – it was what Mr Ellyott said. Wasn't it Mr Ellyott?'

Amos, who had been sitting quiet and watchful, looked suddenly irritable. 'A question of terms, madam.

Perhaps attacked was too strong. I withdraw the word.'

Mrs Edmunds nodded. 'Mr Ellyott paid me a visit.' She almost smiled at him. Then she was off on another tack. 'This woman – Mrs Ridetski. All of you called there, didn't you? I'm not going to comment about that. You're men now. Men have all the privileges, don't they? But – this is what I want to know – the authorities don't really think Marshall had anything to do with this woman's death, do they?'

My turn to answer again. 'Course they don't. It's just that Mash forgets – gets mixed up – sometimes.' Oh God, I thought.

Now she was agitated, restless on the chair, the needles going ever faster. 'He forgets. He forgets because he's got nothing to tell them. Having a father who had to join in this confessing business didn't help. Did you know...?' She choked on the words. 'Did you know he told the police that Marshall slept here in his bed that night?' And he did sleep here – not in his bed granted. But how would he know? Where was he that night? Out exercising as per usual? Delivering bits of paper?' A silence that stretched. Outside on the lawn the swallows flew low. Even the needles were still. Then she resumed, words tumbling out of her, as if her speech were somehow connected to the movement of her hands. 'What does he do? Plays with the boy. They wrestle. Play games. All games with him. All talk, talk, talk.' I was shocked. I wanted to tell her to think what she was saying – to shut up. 'That's why I gave up handing over... Look – it was my money that set him up, but I had to pull out otherwise there would have been nothing. Nothing for the boy.' Whatever reason she might have had for asking us to call this wasn't it, I felt. All this was burning inside her. Had to come out. 'You start asking questions about where he got the money from, Mr Ellyott. He was close to bankruptcy. No more from me, I said. But he kept on going, didn't he? Even with petrol rationed. Even with no cars to sell. You start asking questions. That's all.' Her glasses had steamed up. She ran her finger behind each lens. A dark cloud overhead. Shadows in the room. 'That's all I'm saying. I'm very tired. Please go now.'

I looked at Emlyn. He motioned for me to stand. Amos said, 'But, dear lady, if you could...'

She dismissed us. 'You let yourselves out. Please. The boys know the way.'

I followed Emlyn to the door. Click click click went the needles. Amos came shuffling after us. Then she said, 'Knitting helps me to stop thinking.' And we paused there, uneasy, disturbed, but she said no more, and we went out through the house, the click of the needles following us all the way.

Outside the air was fresh and clean. 'I could murder a pint,' Emlyn said. 'She was talking about old MT!'

'A driven woman,' Amos said. 'Desperate. Concerned with another matter.'

'A man burnt in pound notes,' I said, Mash's voice in my head. We came to a halt. Swallows swooped around us. 'I just thought of that,' I added feebly.

'Philip will insist on playing at detective,' the old man remarked. 'A Sergeant Lockman, of the American Army Pay Corps, with a car full of money, who came to ashes on the coast road...'

'How much money?' I asked him.

'Enough for a bonfire, apparently.'

'Enough to save a man from going bust?'

'Do not anticipate,' Amos said with something that might have been a laugh.

We walked on in silence until we came to the Anchorage, which always tried to be better than it was, and which we never patronised. 'It will have to do,' Amos insisted. But he barred our entrance briefly with his stick. 'Should we not have asked the lady of the house were she was on the night in question?'

'Oh, really, bollocks,' Emlyn told him and went ahead into the pub.

'But the motive is there,' Amos said softly. 'Think about it.'

'Mash? In Lilian's case it might make sense, but what about the others?' He stared at me over his glasses, challenging me to say more. 'To make us think it's a maniac? Draw attention away from Lilian's case?' He nodded encouragingly. 'But – Ridetski, if he's after something would want to do that, wouldn't he?'

'A person resembling Ridetski has been reported in the area, certainly...'

'Well – Ridetski then?'

'Not a desperate and driven lady? A local?' He barked a spiteful laugh at me.

The first thing we heard in the pub was that the police had taken the German in. Everyone heard it. Jack Partridge, doing the rounds, was shouting it out.

'Klaus Schneider – found the keys for the Market Hall on him. All them pissing Nazis should be hung!'

'It will be necessary for us to take a look at Mr George Garston at home,' Amos Ellyott whispered to us across the table. I had never met anyone who wanted to raise his voice above a whisper in the Anchorage, except Jack Partridge, and they had long since called the police to show him the way out. 'Former prisoners of war interest me, of course, but Garston interests me more. Marshall can drive us thither.' Mash, with white from the marking-out machine still on his hands, had joined us after a search that had taken in most of the town's pubs. 'Does not the gentleman live on a farm named Y Gors?'

That style of speaking was bound to bring out the worst in Emlyn. He rolled his eyes at me and said, 'Yea, verily.'

'And this farm – is it not some miles hence?'

'A fair number of leagues, sirrah,' Emlyn said. It had to be the Anchorage that set them going like this. Everyone in it, the barmaid especially, looked stuffed.

'You're not thinking of going now? This time of night?'

'Precisely, Philip. Now. And don't you dare bring me into this wax works again.'

Mash, who had been removing white from under his nails with a matchstick, thought this was very funny.

'Dead of night has great significance for the peasantry,' Amos explained, once we were bouncing along the track that led to George Garston's sour acres. 'Night brings on dread and unease...'

'Oh, Christ,' Emlyn moaned in my ear, 'this is making jelly of my insides. We'll never make it.'

The way to Y Gors twisted like a snake through broom, gorse and marram grass. It was a poor farm on the edge of the estuary, most of its fields sandy and barren and subject to tidal floods – a low-lying, sinister place even in broad daylight. Mash's headlights picked out signs that said 'DANGER' and 'NO WAY' and 'NO SHOOTING'. A dead gull hung from one of them.

'Slow down Mash,' Emlyn cried out, 'I'm having a heart attack.'

But Mash flung the little car at the bends and rode the potholes with abandon, driving badly. Normally he was fast but careful. Now he deemed to misjudge the bends, and I began to wonder how many pints he'd had. The old man was enjoying it, however. We could hear snatches of song from him.

Just before we reached the white gate that guarded the house, Mash must have stamped hard on the accelerator and we went off in a skid, and finished up with the back of the car almost touching the gate.

'I've gone!' Emlyn groaned as we disentangled ourselves. He gave Mash a punch. 'What are you pissing playing at, you bloody great 'nana? I'm damaged, that's what. Had it!'

Mash switched off the engine. Now we could hear George Garston's dogs howling, and music accompanying them. *Tosca*, I think, flooding out of the house behind us. 'Hey that's nice,' Mash said, 'what do we do now?'

Emlyn appeared to be rubbing himself all over, as if attempting to restore circulation. 'We were going to create a diversion so that Mr Ellyott could have a look round. Maybe burn a barn, or stampede Garston's cattle. But you've buggered it up!'

'Oh, I'm sorry,' Mash said.

'That's all right, Emlyn responded, 'Don't let it happen again.'

'Have we landed?' Amos enquired. 'Create a diversion? Stampede cattle? I don't remember saying anything about that. Help me out of this wretched car. I must urinate. Then we'll call on Mr Garston. Philip and I.'

'You do your own calling,' I said to him as we climbed out. We stood in a line and aimed at George

Garston's gate, the old man muttering angrily because he couldn't manage it. The music stopped and we saw the front door of the farm open. The porch light came on, and Garston stood there, a shotgun in his hands.

'Who is out there?' we heard him call. Then he pointed the gun at the sky and fired off one barrel.

'Oh my God,' Emlyn said, 'doesn't he know about my nerves?' The dogs, silenced for a moment by the shot, resumed their howling.

'It is I, Ellyott,' Amos shouted. 'Be so kind as to secure all creatures. I have come to see you.' He motioned me to follow him and pushed the gate open.

'After you,' I said to Emlyn, but he shook his head and said I was to go with the old man, just in case something happened to him because he was liable to snuff it any minute.

'When you've finished discussing my health, we'll proceed,' Amos said sharply.

'You and diversions,' I said to Emlyn as I went through the gate. I was still saying it as we walked across the yard. And God only knew what we were walking in. The whole place stank like a dunghill.

'Unlike Emlyn,' Amos said, 'you have no imagination and no flair. Kindly remember that we are here to create unease; to surprise.'

But the surprises came from Garston. For a start he was wearing a collar and tie and a velvet smoking jacket, with tartan slippers on his feet. For another he stepped forward and gripped Amos's hand and shook it, saying 'This is indeed an honour, Mr Ellyott.'

Then there was the room he led us into. I had expected a farmhouse kitchen, but this was a study, furnished and carpeted and panelled in dark oak. There was a desk big enough for a managing director, three leather armchairs, a filing cabinet, glass-fronted bookcases, and sporting prints on the walls. 'Please be seated,' he urged us. The books were mostly leather-bound volumes, some with Latin titles, and they provided the explanation, I felt. Garston had been around the sales, possibly in a country house somewhere, and this was a job lot. But that didn't account for the jacket. I stared at him as he took his seat behind the desk. I hadn't expected to find George Garston playing at Squire.

He picked up a pen from the silver inkstand on the desk. 'I was listening to great music – *Tosca*,' he said, and I thought he looked uglier than ever without his cap, even balding in an ugly manner. 'Do you like music, Mr Ellyott?' Not once did he acknowledge my presence. Someone stamped on the floor above us. 'Distinguished visitor,' he shouted, then to us in explanation, 'only my son, David, you know, since my wife passed on.' Worked her into the grave, had been Laura's verdict. 'Do you like music, Mr Ellyott?'

'You're a fool, Garston,' Amos said. 'You know quite well we didn't come here to discuss music...'

'Oh, yes – these terrible tragedies in the town?' He looked up, his Adam's apple bobbing as he shouted, 'It's Mr Ellyott, the famous criminologist!'

'Who would be grateful for a drop of gin,' Amos said with a leer.

Garston showed brown and broken teeth. 'You are always welcome in my little house, Mr Ellyott.'

'With a gin, I trust?'

Garston plucked a black hair from his nostril. 'Oh, but I regret to say I don't keep intoxicating spirit in the house. A good temperance family, you see...'

Amos got to his feet. 'In which case, since you do not wish to be hospitable, I'll go.'

Garston jumped up. 'Oh no. Please. I'm very sorry. Perhaps there may be a drop somewhere.' He began to open drawers in the desk. 'Wait. If you please. Excuse me.' He vanished from view behind the desk and we heard the clink of glass and the sound of paper being torn. 'I might have something here, though I never touch a drop myself.'

Amos winked at me.

'Here you are,' he said, breathing heavily as he emerged from behind the desk. 'I hope it will be the right drink.' A half bottle of gin, US Army for the use of. He had, for some reason, torn off the label. It was clear to me then what kind of goods he had stored in the narrow room on the top floor of the Market Hall. 'It was given to me as a present many years ago,' he explained.

Twenty minutes later and very little happened apart from Amos swigging at the gin. Garston had apologised four times for firing off the gun.

'Let us particularise,' Amos said. 'Your keys were stolen?'

'Oh, would you believe it? The first time it's ever happened to me. A whole bunch. All the keys to the properties in which I have a small interest...'

'When were they stolen?'

'Garston made a thinking face. 'Well – it must have been on Saturday afternoon. Us country people, you know – we never lock our doors. Mind you, I never use them keys very much. All my tenants – well, they're not really tenants, more like friends really – they all have their own keys – as part of the contract.'

'Special keys for special locks?'

'Oh – I wouldn't say that. Most of them were ordinary...'

'But some were special – and expensive?'

'Oh – well I wouldn't say that. You see...'

'I would like to see your son,' Amos said briskly, and dipped his nose into his glass.

Now Garston for the first time was alarmed. 'David? But he's at his studies, you see. Learning to be a doctor, see...'

'I would still like to see him.' Amos banged his glass down. 'Not for questions...'

'David can answer any question anybody asks him.' A sudden show of defiance that brought colour to his sallow cheeks. 'He's always at his books...'

'Last Saturday night, too?'

'With me at the concert. He never left my side. People who know me can swear...'

'In which case,' Amos said wearily, 'he has nothing to fear. Be good enough to bring the young man in.' He left the request like a challenge on the air. Garston's eyes flickered, a rapid calculation going on. Then he got up and went out of the room, and Amos turned and gave me a pitying look that said I bet you don't know what I'm up to. And he was right. Senile decay was all I was thinking.

Then we heard David Garston in protest. 'For God's sake – you don't have to lock me in!' Garston ushered him into the room. 'How do you do, Mr Ellyott,' he said stiffly. They had done wonders to his accent at that school. He didn't say anything to me.

'Studying to be a doctor in London,' Garston said.

'Oh, for God's sake, Dad!'

I had forgotten what he looked like and was

surprised to find how short he was. Short and neat – dapper, I thought. And he had a beauty of a black eye.

Amos stood and planted his hat on his head. 'Thank you – that will be all,' he said, and raised a beckoning finger at me.

'You're not going, Mr Ellyott?' Garston was genuinely dismayed. 'Another drink, perhaps?'

'Open the door for me, Philip.' To David Garston he said, 'One more thing. Can you tell me why Marshall Edmunds assaulted you?'

David's hand went to his eye. 'Not a clue,' he said.

'Thank you,' Amos said, 'that will be all. I may want to question you again.'

'I'm always here,' he replied, 'under lock and key.' More than a touch of bitterness, I thought, but like his father he was surprised at his dismissal. 'Just looking, were you, Mr Ellyott?' And I thought good boy, David, more to you that meets the eye.

'David can answer any question anybody can ask him,' Garston said as he escorted us across the yard. 'It's been a great honour for me to have you visit my humble home, Mr Ellyott.' At the gate he said, 'Good night, Philip.'

'Ah, so you knew I was here all the time,' I replied, and Amos muttered 'Bravo'.

Mash, on Emlyn's orders, drove back very slowly, but he picked up another puncture not far from his house and we had to push the car up the drive. 'I'd better give him a hand,' Emlyn said. 'He gets all mixed up.' And once again I was left to look after the old man.

He had been silent in the car, listening to my description of Garston at home at Emlyn's request.

But now as we walked along the dark promenade he talked incessantly. 'One can find reasons for Ridetski leaving his wife,' was his opener, 'but why should he want to leave such a promising little business? Don't interrupt, I am clarity itself in the dark, and please walk straight. You keep on banging into me.'

'It's you,' I told him.

'Nonsense,' he said. 'This Lilian gave her favours to many. How very 'old comrades' of you three young men, home from the wars. How very sophisticated and how naive. In a capital city – London, say, or Paris, – an acceptable arrangement. But here! In this little corner! Such naivety! Don't interrupt. You all liked her – by which I mean you found her amusing. But did one of you like her too much perhaps? Found the arrangement unacceptable – so that one day he all but chokes the life out of his best friend? What do you say to that?'

'You tell me,' I said.

'And why would he do that? Was it because you had both promised not to see her again, and was it because he thought he had seen Emlyn leaving the lady's house?'

'It's a theory,' I agreed.

'It's what you think, Philip. Lilian was free with her favours – not an allegation to be aimed at Miss Porterhouse or Miss Sweeney so far as we know. Men called at Lilian's – and consider this: how easy for a man to make a mistake, a man whose eyes are failing...'

'Whose eyes are failing?'

'Marshall Edmunds. Will you please walk straight? Don't you know Marshall is deteriorating?'

'For Christ's sake!'

‘A deterioration taking place. His eyesight – did you notice the way he drove tonight? Reactions slowing down.’ I shook his arm away. ‘Listen to me! You know it as well as I do. Deterioration. In the end he will withdraw entirely. His mother knows that...’

‘Well for God’s sake, Mash didn’t kill her – or anybody!’

‘That remains to be seen. But isn’t it possible that he might have mistaken David Garston for Emlyn?’

‘David Garston?’

‘On a darkened street? His sight less sharp? Isn’t it possible? The same build, the same colouring?’ We had reached Ocean View. I helped him up the stairs to his door. He tapped his stick against my fly so that I backed away hastily. ‘The trouble that thing causes. Young Mr Garston was also a visitor. George Garston would not have liked that, would he?’ He reached for his key above the door. ‘Such a concealed man. The doctor to be dallying with a fallen woman. Enough to bring on a frenzy, would you think?’ He opened the door and stepped inside, then poked his head out to say, ‘think about it, Philip. And if the police stop you on your way home just mention my name.’

I walked across a deserted town, hoot of sirens in my ears, and pondered. They must have had the entire force on night duty. I was stopped four times and questioned, and none of them had even heard of Amos Ellyott.

Laura was waiting up for me. ‘I want to lock up for myself,’ she said, ‘then I’ll know it’s safe. Mind you – I think we’re all right. It’s only these strangers who get killed... Are you thinking about something, Philip?’

‘Good God,’ I said, ‘does it show?’

X

On the morning of MT's sports day there was a deluge, and at eleven still no break in the clouds. Eleven was a special hour, according to Laura – rain at eleven meant rain for the rest of the day, because of the tides.

I found Ceri out shopping and took her to Bodawen's cafe for a cup of coffee. 'He'll have to cancel it,' she said, 'or turn it into a swimming gala. Anyway, my father says that a malaise has come to town. That's how he talks all the time. In metaphor.' She dabbed some of the skin from the coffee off her upper lip. She had a beautiful, full mouth. 'My mother takes great comfort from the fact that the victims are all new, not natives like us.' She had a slow way of speaking that I found appealing. 'But we sleep with all the bedroom doors open so we can call for help if he comes to the wrong house.' She smiled. 'Shouldn't joke, though, should I? It's panic stations. All over town. That poor old girl yesterday. It was even on the wireless this morning. The Police keep on telling Dad everything's under control, inquiries proceeding; arrest imminent. All that. But old Mr Ellyott says this kind of killer is the most difficult to catch – no motive, or something. And there's talk, Philip.'

'What about?'

'You three.' She gave me a long, searching look. 'About old Mash, especially...'

'Why pick on Mash?'

'I'm just telling you.'

'Just because he's got problems? That doesn't make him...'

'Don't get rattled!'

'Have you been told not to see me, then?'

'I see who I like, Philip Roberts.' And we had a long and angry silence which she ended by buttoning her mac and pulling her hat over her ears. 'Back to the piano,' she said, and she leaned across the table and kissed me. 'Come on. Walk me home.'

Outside her house she said, 'I can't see you tonight. Not because of what you're thinking. I've got some girls coming over for the evening.' I looked up at the house and saw a curtain shift back into place. 'But call for me here tomorrow – OK?' I said I'd do that, and walked away and saw her face in all the puddles in the street.

'You're too deep for me, Philip,' Idwal Morton said. 'It's all foolosophy where I'm concerned, not that deep stuff. But I suppose you're right – wars change you. Though I missed them both.'

He sat very still at the cluttered kitchen table, the paper open at the racing page. 'Yes sir. I've given up thinking.' He ticked a horse. 'It'll all be the same in a million years.' A train went by and he winced. 'They let the German chappie go this morning. At least they were talking of letting him go. They haven't got a clue; useless all of them – how d'you mean, you can't remember?'

'About how it was before the war. I can remember when I'm told – when somebody starts talking. Like Emlyn does...'

Idwal smiled grimly. 'Oh, he remembers it all.'

'But when I start thinking about it myself, I can't remember.'

'Anything in particular you want to remember?'

No I said, I didn't think so. Idwal stared hard at the newspaper, tapping it gently with his pencil. 'When I was young,' he said, 'I was going to be a world beater. I used to walk around thinking I could do anything.' He spoke always as if he didn't expect to be heard. 'You learn you can't.' He looked at me then, a light in his deep-set eyes but no change in his voice. 'You're the strong one of the three. They listen to you. Tell Emlyn to stop pushing it, all right?'

'Pushing what?'

Idwal looked up. 'God, what is he doing up there? Takes him a day to comb his hair! Now he was picked up last night. Near the prom. Dressed himself up as a woman! Had a bloody steel bar this long under his arm! Decoy he says! Now you tell him to stop messing about.'

Emlyn came in. 'Three guesses who you're talking about,' he said. Then, to his father, 'Beg your pardon – we're not speaking today are we?'

'You are a stupid bastard,' I said to him.

'In retrospect, I agree. They were not amused.'

'Why don't you write them a letter and ask to be bloody well locked up?'

'Granted, granted. But it might have worked.' His face broke into a wide, cheeky smile. 'You've got to take chances, though I was shit scared all the time. By the way, the Inspector is very anxious to have a word with you.'

'Me? What about?'

'Yours truly,' Emlyn said, 'I should think.'

Inspector Marks came out of his car on the High Street and called me over. He looked even more at the point of exhaustion than he had done the last time I'd seen him. A worn old face above a crisp white shirt. 'I'll come straight to the point,' he said as we stood out of the rain in a shop doorway. 'I've spoken to Emlyn Morton, who is very lucky not to be behind bars even if he was a hero in the war. We can tolerate no interference. The eye of the nation is on us.' And he went on like that for quite some time. 'There must be discipline. We know what we're doing.' He sighed deeply. 'But – above all else – please keep that old man out of my way...'

'Mr Ellyott? I'm not in charge of him.'

He gripped his brow. 'Please,' he said, 'please. I look to you for discretion, so keep this to yourself.' He looked around to see if we were likely to be overheard. 'They kicked him out. Long ago. For malpractice, I understand. Do you follow me? Please – without saying anything to him directly, keep him out of my hair, I beg of you. This is not a comedy. I cannot face waking up to another day of him!'

'I've no chance,' I said.

'I know.' He nodded sadly. 'I simply thought I'd ask.'

Coronation Park had been a gift to the town by the same lady who had left it with King Teddy's statue. It had been opened with a flourish in 1911 with a flying display, but the plane had failed to clear the fences surrounding the ground. Thereafter it had had its ups and downs. Mainly downs. Now it bore the scars of its occupation during the war as a parking area for military vehicles, its tennis courts fissured, the football pitch covered in waist high grasses. The pavilion had lost part of its roof and its windows were boarded over. MT came blundering down the steps from the veranda to greet us, and his foot went through. 'Halloo my bonny laddies,' he called to us as he heaved himself free. 'Not a bad sort of day, is it? Could be worse – eh?' The rain overhung the park like a shroud – dense, placing limits on visibility.

Amos Ellyott was sitting on the veranda, a blanket over his knees and an umbrella open above his head. He was talking to Ceri's father, a short and remote man staring at nothing through thick horn-rims. Inside the pavilion there were two dozen or more children, already wet, most of them involved in fights.

'We are quite booked up for the junior races,' MT declared, 'but we have nobody for the senior events.'

'They are pretending your sports day isn't happening,' Ceri's father surprised us by saying. 'This town – it has a genius for turning the blind eye. Even on murders. Nasty things do not happen here – not that your sports are in any sense nasty, of course.'

'The hundred yards,' MT went on, glancing at us meaningfully. 'We must do something...'

'Put us down.' Emlyn volunteered, and clapped a hand over my mouth to stop any protest. 'It'll be a laugh,' he smiled. MT went off clapping with delight.

'Out there?' I said. MT and Mash had rough cut a rectangular section for the track – it looked like a short landing strip in a jungle, and was brown and obviously water logged. 'You must be out of your tiny mind.'

Emlyn was kneeling at a little boy's feet, tying up his laces. 'Mash is going to run,' he reasoned, 'therefore Mash has to have someone to run against.' He looked up at me. 'Got it?'

'In the first place I've no kit,' I said. 'In the second place I can't run anyway.' The little boy, who had straight red hair and evil eyes, held a pair of tiny football shorts towards me and I knew I was beaten.

Emlyn smiled up at him. 'What's your name?'

'Captain X,' the boy replied. He turned and looked up in admiration, and I knew Mash had come in.

Mash was wearing shorts and a vest and carried a pair of spiked running shoes. 'Tarzan,' Captain X said in a whisper, and the children came crowding. Mash flexed his muscles for them, grabbed Sian Thomas and held her high, then gently lowered her to the floor and placed his huge hand on the crown of her head.

'After the next shower,' MT announced, 'we'll make a start.' He began to take their names and ages. Captain X told him he could be seven or eleven; didn't matter to him. 'Astonishing,' MT said, 'but willing. Now, the band will be here in a minute and we'll soon see the atmosphere buck up. How is the weather?'

'Pissing down,' an answer that came from a small boy named Robert Owen who had the frozen face of a practised ventriloquist. I looked out across the veranda. There was no other word for it.

At half past two the Brynbach Silver Band sent word that they would not be arriving owing to the inclement weather being bad for their tubes. They were all in the King's Arms, the messenger reported, and had been there for some time. 'Never mind,' MT sighed. Ceri's father wondered if it was all really appropriate, given the time and the occasions and the place and didn't MT think that it would be better perhaps to abandon the sports. 'Not until three,' MT said firmly. 'We never gave up until three in the old days.'

At three o'clock a halt to the downpour arrived and the sports day began. But after only a few races it became out of control. Each race became a swim and discipline broke down. Soon the clothes of each participant clung to them, and they revelled in it and kicked off their shoes and took no heed of the starter's whistle or finishing tape. Now and then we had to go and rescue them from the deep water–logged ruts made by the army wagons long ago. Seven of them set out on a run, but only three returned. The rest we found among the tall grasses, hunting for tadpoles in an oily pool. 'Not to worry,' said MT, 'everything is going very well.'

We poured hot tea into the children and wrapped them up between races with the towels MT had brought along, feeding them buns and cakes. 'Be kind enough to bring me a list of suspected winners,' Ceri's father said to MT, 'I have an appointment with the spokesman for the police.' And he went marching off, shaking his head sadly.

'Everything is going splendidly,' MT assured us, patting his blazer pockets. 'Looking for his whistle,' Emlyn whispered. 'I saw Captain X hiding it under a brick behind the pavilion. What a great bloody day!'

We stood side by side for the hundred yards, Mash in full running kit, Emlyn dapper in a pair of shorts and vest and me with my trousers rolled up to the knees, my shirt flapping. The children lined the track which was now like a swamp. 'Ready, steady, off,' MT cried out. Mash and Emlyn were away before I realised it was time to go, and after only a few skidding paces I was down. I watched the race through a curtain of grass. Emlyn stayed with him all the way, the children whooping and screaming, and Mash was only a close winner.

I was helped to my feet, brushed down by sympathetic hands. Emlyn came back blowing hard. 'You wait,' he said between gulps of air, 'I'll run him into the ground in the 400 – even if I have to suffer tomorrow.'

MT came up to me as I sat on the veranda wringing out my socks. 'We carried on, Philip. Remember that. In spite of everything we carried on, yesterday and today, set in motion the revival of our little town. You remember don't you, what a great place it used to be during the season?' I nodded. Speech was out of the question. 'You know,' he went on, lowering his voice, 'if I had to leave here – this town – I'd die. Only here can I really be.' I heard the click of knitting needles in my ears. 'I would do anything rather than leave this place. Excuse me – I am running in the 400 as well.'

Amos Ellyott was staring at me over his glasses. 'Even the simplest of men can be aroused,' he said. Mash was surrounded by small boys, distributing cake and pop. Emlyn was towelling a little girl's hair, and talking to her, and she was close to wetting herself with laughter. Sunlight came in huge shafts of white. A thrush sang. 'I hear someone answering Ridetski's description was seen in the railway station lavatories two days ago. Did you know Emlyn Morton's father was notorious for his violence as well as his womanising?' Shut up, old man, I said to myself. 'Philip, we are going to look for a single tower on a hill. I have come into possession of a photograph.'

'Photo of what?'

The old man frowned. 'Must you be so dense? A

tower, one solitary tower on a hill.'

'Here we are,' MT cried out as he came bounding. He was wearing khaki shorts that hid his knees, a vest and tennis shoes. 'Mr Ellyott – as a special favour – could I prevail on you to act as starter?' The old man was agreeable but it took some time to get him to his feet and unlock his joints. But once on the field, still with his umbrella open above his head, he was suspiciously nimble.

'You're enjoying it too,' Emlyn said to him.

'Yes, but will I be here when you return?' he replied.

I managed to stay on my feet during that race, but I finished last. Mash won by a short head from Emlyn. MT had to lie down to recover, his face puce, his eyes rolling. We had to give him the fireman's lift back to the pavilion. 'Line up everybody, for presentations,' he gasped. 'Then we'll have the English, followed by "Land of my Fathers..."'

This was the part he really loved. The ceremony, the handshaking, a few words of encouragement and congratulation, a prize for everyone, then 'God Save the King', and he standing there to attention, long khaki shorts clinging wetly to thin white legs. Emlyn and Mash stood on either side of him watching the children at song, smiling at each other. Oh, Jesus, Jesus, I was surrounded by boys. And at that moment Robert Owen and Captain X, who hadn't claimed their prizes, came running from the park screaming 'there's a lady in the grass!'

'God save the King' died on a note. We were all running up the track towards the tall grasses where the boys stood pointing. Emlyn, head back, went past me in a spurt. 'You've got to stop them!' he cried out. 'Quickly – the kids!' I had no idea what he intended, but I found some speed from somewhere and caught up with him, and the three of us turned, arms outstretched to face the children. They came running at us. 'No further,' Emlyn yelled, and they came to a tumbling halt and looked at us wide eyed and wondering. Behind them, hobbling slowly, MT was on his way, Amos Ellyott on his arm.

'That's it!' Emlyn roared. 'It's a joke, see. Now – first to pass me and Mash gets half a crown. All right?' He waited for a few nods, then he pointed towards the pavilion. 'This is for the real championship. Are you ready?' Then he was off, Mash at his side, and the children went whooping after them.

I turned to Robert Owen and Captain X, who stood at the edge of the tall grass, like Indian scouts, pointing. 'In there,' Robert Owen said, and suddenly I was in a rage and bawled at them to stay where they were and went stamping into the grass, sweeping it aside, not feeling the wetness of it. 'Long way in,' I heard Robert Owen call, and I was knee deep in brimming ruts, and swearing, ready to take on anybody, anytime. Until I saw the flowered dress, a ringlet of drowned hair with mud on it.

I was for going back to call the Inspector, and to hell with it. But I parted the grasses and took a closer look. A ragged remnant of floral cotton. A doll's head, eyeless. I reached for it but couldn't bring myself to touch it. All I could do was crouch there, staring.

MT and the old man came up behind me. 'Having us on,' he said. 'The damn young rascals.'

'Now it's a game for children,' I heard Amos Ellyott say.

XI

I went home and turned on the gas boiler and took a long bath. By the time I was changing into dry clothes I was thinking of it as a bad joke, nothing more. With corpses popping up all over the place who could blame Captain X and Robert Owen for taking the mickey? As I pulled on clean socks, I thought of little Miss Porterhouse on the King's stony lap, Miss Sweeney among the flowers – no need for me to be touched, and my apologies to you Captain X and frozen-faced Robert Owen for bawling you out... but Lilian was different. Not a game for children. I had known Lilian.

The back door opened and I could hear Laura's voice, Will Wilkins too. A conversation that rose through the joists – they were both loud speakers.

'No more of those murders today, thank goodness,' Laura said.

'Don't you worry your head, my dear. Ask yourself – who were these women? Not real people of the town, were they? Not like you and me...'

'The people in the hall – that's what they said – but it doesn't sound quite right, does it...?'

'These strangers.' Will Wilkins strangled the letter "r". 'It's got nothing to do with our kind of life. Where did they come from? Who do they belong to?'

'That old war. Mollie Ann Fruits said that's what brought them here.'

'If it was one of our real community it would be different,' Will Wilkins declared. And there was a long silence during which I became conscious that I was eavesdropping. Then Laura's voice came through, 'Mr Wilkins! Cheeky boy!' And suddenly she was squealing and it sounded as if old Wilkins was chasing her around the kitchen. 'Ow!' she cried, 'you've bust my strap!'

I decided to creep out, and with all that racket going on there was no need to tiptoe. But Laura must have heard me, and there she was at the passage door, cheeks flushed, her hat askew on her head, one hand at the buttons of her blouse. 'Philip!' she cried out.

'Tut, tut, tut,' I said. She came after me to the front door and caught my arm. 'Philip,' she whispered, 'don't make fun of me. His intentions are honourable.' But nothing could wipe the smile off my face. 'That old shop – not making enough to keep it going, Philip.' She managed the button at last, but her strap had gone and she had her elbow up for support. 'I've got to think of the future. Only what your father left, and not so much of that.' It was painful trying not to laugh, the two of us standing there in the gloom by the front door. 'He'll be speaking to you – I expect,' she went on. 'Oh, don't laugh at me, Philip. Your father always laughed at me.' Real hurt in her voice. I was able to mumble something – I don't know what – and didn't laugh when her hat dipped over one eye as she opened the door for me.

Out on the street I found myself thinking about my father – as he was in that photograph in the album; his grey bowler, the carnation in his button hole, the long cigarette holder, the pearl pin in his tie, the waxed moustache. A dandy among his books and musical friends. J. Palmer Roberts. Always an old man to me. And how for a long summer I had hated him for bringing Laura into the house. Never her. But him. For a whole summer... It was years since I had thought of it, a long summer's hating when I was thirteen and I could scarcely believe that it had been so, remembering him now with such affection.

They were waiting for me in the King's Arms, Mash and the old man and Emlyn. On the way there I had seen MT and Idwal Morton deep in conversation under the beech trees by the station, and I wasn't the only one who was surprised when they followed me into the pub. 'Hey Mash – Our Father's which art in public houses...' Emlyn said. 'Don't tell me he's going back on the juice.' But Idwal had a glass of soda water at his elbow. I saw him watch MT down a whiskey and saw him insist on paying for the next one. There was a kind of weary disdain in everything Idwal did. They made a striking contrast, the one so hearty, the other so worn.

Drinks arrived from them. 'Just so long as they don't join us,' Emlyn said as he waved our thanks. 'This afternoon did me a great deal of harm – deep down. Two hours I had in the bath. Had a dizzy turn later.'

'The kids were great,' Mash said.

'Should have called them up for the war,' Emlyn remarked, 'as a civilising influence.' He touched Amos's arm. 'Are you all right, Mr Ellyott?'

The old man shivered. 'Thought I was going then,' he mumbled, and dipped his nose quickly into the gin.

MT left. Idwal Morton came over but refused a

chair. 'Why should I watch you lot drink yourselves to death?' he said. 'They tell me they let the German go. Quite right too – he couldn't knock the skin off a rice pudding, that one. They say he used to clean out the hairdressers for her on a Sunday morning...'

'Quite so, quite so.' The old man dismissed the subject. 'Please be kind enough to tell me where this might be.' He took a photograph, well over postcard size, from his pocket and placed it on the table.

Idwal leaned over my shoulder, a smell of old fags coming from him. 'Wright's Tower,' he said. 'Over on Morwyn hill.' It was a photograph taken in late evening: a steep valley, a road curling over a bridge, and above the valley the Tower flanked by tall trees, dark against the sky. Idwal reached for it, examining the back as well. 'Where did you get this, Mr Ellyott?'

Amos was quite sharp with him. 'Why – has it any significance?'

'Mr Wright's Tower,' Idwal said slowly. He dropped the photograph on the table. Emlyn picked it up and showed it to Mash. I could feel Idwal's hand trembling on my shoulder. 'Mr Wright was rich. He must have thought the district required some improvement. It's a folly, that Tower. The Celtic twilight must have got to him, don't you think?' Idwal's familiar, sardonic tones brought on a silence. 'The scene of an accident, too.' He went on: 'Just past the bridge there...'

'Where an absconding Sergeant of the Americans died in a furnace of money,' Amos said. 'In 1942. I know, I know.' He snatched the photograph from Emlyn's hand and stuffed it in his pocket, and I wondered why the old coot should suddenly be so irritable.

'Mr Wright's dead too,' Idwal said, lightly. 'I used

to hold the grazing rights to that land. In better days. Now, let me buy you a drink...'

'I'm much obliged to you, Mr Morton – for your explanation and the offer.' Then he looked up at Idwal and smiled. 'Please excuse my rudeness. You see someone took it upon themselves to send me this photograph through the post and without a word of explanation. It annoys me. I think it came from behind a strip of wallpaper in Mrs Ridetski's house.'

After a silence Idwal said: 'That would make it a clue, then?' Amos laughed and I heard Idwal laugh lightly with him. 'Why don't you ask Emlyn here? He's a good wallpaper stripper...'

'Not to take the piss, father,' Emlyn said. 'Stand aside – I'll get the drinks.'

Amos brought his fist down hard on the table and set the glasses tinkling. 'Someone in this town is playing games,' he growled. 'Someone thinks I'm an idiot. A photograph through my letter box! Who do they think I am?' He was staring at Idwal Morton. 'Someone is trying to lay a false trail.' The whole pub could hear him. 'I am not used to being trifled with. Whoever is fooling about is fooling about with the wrong man.' He sat back after that, muttering to himself, ticking like a time bomb.

'Well,' Emlyn said with a nervous laugh, 'I'll be getting the drinks...'

'You sit down,' Idwal said, and he went over to the bar and called out the order.

The old man shook his head. 'Oh my word, I had a funny turn then.' He took the drink from the tray Idwal held out to him. 'Your very good health. Had a funny turn then. I felt as if I had gone – beyond.' He cocked an eyebrow at Idwal. 'You serve an excellent gin, steward. My word, what a funny turn.'

Idwal wished us good night, and as the others started to discuss the sports day once more I sat back and watched Amos Ellyott, and wondered what he was playing at. Why that pantomime all of a sudden? Was Idwal Morton on the list of suspects, too?

'We'll go now,' he announced suddenly.

Emlyn choked over his drink. 'Go where?'

'Wright's Tower,' Amos said. 'We've been invited.'

Morwyn Hill and the Tower Mr Wright had built were on the old coast road out of the town, a swinging, dipping track no longer a highway, and wide enough for only one car. Mash drove very carefully, Emlyn whispering in his ear. When we reached the crest of the steepest hill Amos ordered him to stop.

'There you are,' he announced. 'The photograph in its entirety. Pause at the bridge, Marshall. I wish to observe the scene of the accident.'

On the bridge he opened a window and stuck his head out, shielding his eyes against the evening sun that had finally appeared to mock MT's sports day. 'There,' he said. 'Look.' Below the road, five years on, bits of rusted metal were still visible in the grass.

'Are we going to have a look?' Emlyn suggested.

'To the Tower,' Amos ordered, 'before night comes.'

Emlyn liked that kind of talk. He was sitting up like a boy on a Sunday school trip, chattering about coming here on bikes in the old days.

Half way up the hill Mash turned off along a cart track. A gate barred our way, and there was a field to cross to the rocky outcrop on which the tower stood. We helped Amos out, heaved him over the gate to Mash and walked on. Emlyn was in the lead, still talking, as if set for something exciting. What, I wondered, could Wright's old Tower possibly have to offer? And what did Mash think of all this, never with much to say, less and less now, surely, than before?

We stood below the Tower. It was perhaps thirty feet or more in height, about half that in diameter – built as a ruin and complete with slits for arrows and weathering badly. Names had been scratched in the stone: I wondered if mine was among them. 'Please climb up,' Amos ordered. I indicated that I had left my climbing gear at home. 'Philip, please – you and Emlyn are nimbler. Marshall shall stay with me. I wish to know what is within.' I went on protesting, but Emlyn was already half way up and I said what the hell and followed him. It was an easy climb, footholds in the crumbling mortar gouged out by generations of Maelgwyn's children.

'Christ, it smells like a crow's toilet,' Emlyn said as I perched next to him on the rim. 'Just look at us – puffed out with booze and fags, sitting on this bloody monument on a Saturday night! Mind your pants, everything's dripping with eagle shit!'

Amos called up to us. 'Be so kind as to go down inside this monstrosity. Tell me what you can see.'

'After you, sir,' Emlyn said, 'I'm liable to catch a fowl pest.' We argued, the old man stamping irritably below us and talking about the light going, and I knew we would never hear the end of it if one of us didn't go, and I went gingerly down inside the Tower.

'Cooee!' I yelled through one of the slits.

Amos came into view. 'What are you standing on?' he enquired.

'The floor, what else?' I replied.

'The material,' he said. 'Touch it. Judge if it is more recent than the stone.'

Oh, God, I thought, a tomb! I knelt very slowly. I touched the floor. Concrete. A dead crow lying on it. And something else. A wreath of artificial poppies from an Armistice Day ceremony with a card attached. I could just decipher it: 'To a brave warrior'. I could hear Emlyn laughing above me.

'Philip,' the old man called but I didn't answer him. I was half way up, my fingers scratching for a hold.

'Steady on!' Emlyn cried. 'You'll break your bloody neck!' I reached the top and swung one leg over the rim, and Emlyn was laughing his head off. Until the shot came. A single crack. The whine of a bullet. I nearly fell back into the Tower.

Then Mash was shouting down below, and Emlyn scrambling down, and the old man was lying, crumpled and still, his head bare, his face hidden.

Emlyn was kneeling at the old man's side. 'What's up with him?' Mash was saying. 'Did you hear that bang?' Rooks and crows were circling in disturbed flight. I clambered down and ran, head lowered to them.

'Get down!' Amos ordered. 'All of you!' We pulled Mash to his knees. 'He got my hat. I am unscathed, and thank you for asking.'

'Someone took a pot shot at you,' Emlyn said.

'No need to underline the incident,' Amos snapped back. 'I was the target. I felt the wind of it.'

'It'll be some kid out shooting crows,' I said.

Amos turned his face clear of the crook of his arm. His glasses were at the very tip of his nose. 'I have lived through situations like this,' he told me sharply. 'It was no child with a pea shooter.'

'Oh balls,' Emlyn said. 'The point is where did he fire from?' He looked eagerly at me. 'Tell you what, you go round that way, and I'll go through the trees...'

'No way,' I told him. 'And you're not going either.'

Amos elbowed himself up from the ground. 'It came from the wood over there.'

'Come on, Philip. Two against one. We can get round to him easy.' Emlyn was on his knees, ready to go.

'I order you to stay. Both of you.' Amos spoke with great authority. 'My hat. Retrieve it, if you please.'

Emlyn went scrambling like a crab for it and brought it back. He poked a finger through a hole in the crown and gave a long, low whistle. Amos grabbed it from him and clamped it on his head. An old hat of faded green velvet. I had seen Amos wearing it many times. There had always been a tear in the crown.

Then the second shot came, a singing bullet, then another. We were faces to the ground, stretched out from a common centre like a clock with four fingers. I heard the smack of a rook's body in the grass and black feathers came floating down from the tree above us.

'We've got to go and get him, Philip,' Emlyn said, but he made no move. Mash had caught one of the feathers in the palm of his hand and was examining it carefully, a smile on his face.

'Cigarette,' Amos ordered. 'We stay here. The light is dying.' Emlyn got a cigarette going and we lit up from his. 'Our friend is an embellisher,' Amos remarked softly. 'He must always add another little touch.'

'Supposing he comes belting through the bushes, pumping lead at us?' Emlyn said.

'No, no, no. It is a conversation,' the old man sighed. 'He is talking to us with his gun. He is saying, keep away.'

'From what?'

Amos's cigarette had gone out. He flipped it against the tip of his nose. 'From Wright's tower – wouldn't you think, Philip?'

'He's playing cowboys,' I said. 'He's telling us the Tower is important.'

'Well, well,' the old man said through his cigarette, 'Philip is thinking... So the person who sent me a photograph also fired at us seconds ago?' I was watching Mash as Amos spoke. What the hell did he make of all this? And what the hell were we playing at – lying flat out on this rock, chatting, waiting until some trigger-happy marksman packed away his toy and went home for supper? Another shot. Down went our heads. Beech leaves came tumbling. Good God, I was straight out of the army and I had no idea what to do. A partridge went by overhead, like an express coming out of a tunnel and my face was flat against the stone, and Amos laughed. 'Tell me what disturbed you in the tower,' he asked.

The light was fading fast. In the distance I could see Maelgwyn's lights coming on. 'The concrete looked new on the floor,' I said, not looking at any of them. 'There was a wreath of poppies in there. With a card. "To a brave warrior." Something like that.' And there was a long silence during which I heard a cuckoo from somewhere down in the valley. Near where the wreckage of the car lay, I thought.

'Let us talk about Ridetski,' Amos said after a while. 'Did you know he was employed in the photographic section of the Royal Air Force? A round peg in a round hole: Leading Aircraftsman Ridetski was an expert photographer, and what is more an enthusiastic one, which does not always follow. And in pursuit of his hobby he used Air Ministry facilities for developing and printing. He even used Air Ministry paper...'

'He took the picture you've got?' I asked.

'Do not anticipate,' he gave me a mean look. 'I am offering an hypothesis only.'

Emlyn smiled at me. He had very small, even teeth, and smiling made him look younger than ever. 'I once suffered from a hypothesis...' he said.

Amos chuckled deep in his throat. 'Now, consider this, since we have nothing better to do than to remain prone here until darkness comes. Consider an absconding Sergeant of the American Army Pay Corps, on the run to some girl perhaps in one of the big cities. In his car mail bags crammed with notes, a considerable sum apparently – the pay centre in Plas Beuno down the coast served the numerous American units. And he takes that bend too rapidly, and then briefly he is airborne, somersaulting through the night, and then he is in an incinerator of his own making. Did the doors burst open as the petrol tank exploded? The mail bags – did they fly out clear of the fire?' He paused. The darkness was settling in around us. 'Let us not, however, indulge in too much fancy. Let us stick to facts. Not a note survived the blaze, but there were a number of metal rings which might have come from mail bags. Money burns well. Some of the money, clearly, went up in smoke. But was it all burnt?' He looked over his glasses, first at me, then at Emlyn, then back to me.

'Well – go on,' Emlyn urged him.

'This is not story time,' he said sharply. 'I am outlining a general...' He waved a bony hand on the air.

'I know – but go on.' Emlyn had his face cupped in his hands. A lock of black hair had fallen across his forehead and I noticed for the first time how his hairline was receding. Nothing like lying flat on your face on a lump of rock for making you pay attention to detail. Mash had his huge hands in front of his face, the fingers entwined, and now and then he blew through them softly, owl hoots. Oh Christ, Mash was lost.

'Consider then our Polish photographer, a fastidious and artistic man, whose long absences in the dark room or on photographic jaunts cause much domestic bickering. Violent quarrels in fact.' Amos flipped his unlighted cigarette against his nose. 'Did he walk these fields perhaps with his camera at the ready?' I said, ah, and he told me not to anticipate. 'He photographed birds in their habitat. Was he, perhaps, on his way home from such an expedition when the Sergeant's car failed to negotiate the bend down there? And was there someone else in these fields that night? Someone who came running to the blaze? Someone who intended rescue but was forced to retreat from the flames and who found mailbags, scattered about and clutched them to him, and opened one perhaps...' Once more he waved a fragile hand on the air, like a conductor inviting an orchestra to respond. 'When the firemen and the police arrived there was no-one here. Had Ridetski stolen away too, film in his camera that was to prove a passport from a dingy lodging to a little business?' And he made the ticking noise, *tk, tk, tk.* Making a story of it, I thought.

'Blackmail then?' I said. 'But Ridetski could have taken the money...'

'It is my hypothesis,' he spat back at me, and he lapsed into a sulky silence.

'Makes sense, Philip,' Emlyn remarked. 'You've got to admit...'

I lost my temper. The night air was cool, the stones under me cold, and how absurd to be spending a Saturday night flat out like this just in case someone took another pot shot at us, listening to the senile ramblings of this old codger. 'Listen,' I said, 'you forget about Lilian; you forget about those old girls. Of course Ridetski could have taken the money. Hidden it somewhere. Come back for it, and maybe Lilian had snatched the lot, so he kills her – and then kills the other two to make it look as if there's a maniac about.' A flat silence met this outburst, and I was thinking it sounded like something out of a boys' comic.

'We may stand now,' Amos said, and he ordered us to lift him to his feet. It was some time before he announced that he was mobile, and I wondered at myself for feeling that this was all part of an act with him. But Emlyn fussed around him, 'Don't know about you,' he said, 'but my circulation's packed in entirely.'

'We are safe now,' Amos declared. 'I doubt if he can see the Tower let alone us. Marshall – your arm if you please.' He set off in the direction of the car, hanging on to Mash.

'You go first,' Emlyn said. 'In my state of health even a passing bullet could prove fatal...'

'What do you think – all this burning car and a man taking pictures and somebody getting away with the loot?'

The old man and Mash had come to a halt. 'All bollocks,' Emlyn said. 'Fascinating you've got to admit

– but he's just supposing...'

'I heard that,' Amos growled. 'I would have you know that I have gained an international reputation for just supposing.' Then he warned us to be silent in case the marksman was still around.

There wasn't a marksman, I wanted to say. With this old man it was the way he put words to a situation. We reached the gate and hoisted him over. No one had interfered with the car. We climbed in, Amos insisting, in spite of our protests, that he sit with me at the back. 'I require Philip's company,' he said savagely and we set off. Emlyn and Mash sang the old song 'Queenie' and the old man made laughing noises at my side.

As we neared the town he gripped my arm and spoke into my ear, 'so you wouldn't say Ridetski's in the Tower, Philip?'

'I don't know where the hell he is,' I replied.

'Someone thinks he's in the tower, though.' His long nose was cold against my ear. 'Don't you agree?'

XII

I woke up at ten, sunlight from the window warm across my legs. I reached for my cigarettes to help the questions along but decided against them. We had crashed the last hour of the dance at the Royal, and Emlyn – blowing so badly that he feared his annual attack of asthma was on its way – had given the three piece band a lift, and had got Mash and me into the band's party afterwards. I had a mouth like the bottom of a parrot's cage, physical conditions not conducive to a spell of reasoning, yet the questions came flitting at me like bats in the dark, and as evasive, not making contact, producing no answers. Ridetski. Behind it all the shadow of the Polish airman. If Ridetski had fired the shots why had he done so? To warn us off? To invite us to investigate the tower? Or was Ridetski buried in the Tower, and was this the marksman's way of telling us? And that wreath of poppies, the photograph too – were they all part of the same message? Ridetski killed by the man who had found the money? Lilian too? Had she continued with demands for money? And were little Miss Porterhouse and Miss Sweeney a blind, an invitation to make false assumptions? Oh, brilliant, Philip Roberts... Question makes question, and the wrong set of questions at that. Two things I knew for certain. One was that all that land, Wright's Tower included, freehold and forever, was now part of George Garston's empire. Gareth Williams had told me in the Royal, adding swiftly, 'And how did he get on so quick while us boys was away in the war, then?' The second wasn't a fact, but I was prepared to lay money that old crotchety, arrogant, irritating Amos Ellyott had received more than one photograph – otherwise how would he know about a Polish photographer wandering the fields at night with his camera at the ready? I reached for the cigarettes. That line of reasoning had only brought me back to questions once again.

Laura came in smiling from chapel. 'What a lovely morning,' she said, 'and just think – nobody was murdered at all last night.'

On the way to the boat I met Ceri and arranged to see her that evening. 'Did you know it's in the *News of the World*?' she said. 'Miss Sweeney left all her money to a home for stray cats.' She was wearing a yellow dress, her arms bare and brown, and there were tiny freckles on her nose. 'To the woods,' I suggested, and she said 'Down Rover!' – her piano was waiting.

Emlyn and Mash were stripped off and working when I arrived. Emlyn called me an idle bugger and set me to caulking the forward part of the deck because it was time we stopped fooling about and got the *Ariadne* ready for the blue water. In the same breath he shocked me by saying that he had decided to give Percy Davies Auctioneers another try. 'Don't look so mortified,' he said. 'Everything's getting too bloody bizarre round here. I need some ordinary living for a change. Nine till five.' What about the trumpet? I said. What about the offer from the man who ran the big band up in the port? What about the voyage south? 'We'll fit everything in.'

He assured me. 'But I need some ordinary stuff first – just to see if it's as bad as I remember.' Then he smiled. 'Besides – if I don't sign up for old Percy I won't be in a position to tell him to fuck his job when I go, will I?'

I went up on deck wondering if the reason couldn't be money. Emlyn had been home much longer, and Idwal Morton, they said, had gone through everything – 'From rustling to rags', as he put it – in disastrous litigation not to mention enormous miscalculations in business and far too many years on the bottle. I knelt on the deck and began caulking. This old cow wasn't going to dip her nose into the Mediterranean, was she? Had I ever believed she would? Dreamboat... We'd been playing around, the three of us, celebrating our survival... I looked along the river at the town spread out there beyond the sand hills, tatty old town, a washed-up mess, shut-faced, old stone not married to the new – a place I would have to leave. '"Summer has a fine warm face",' I heard Mash call out below me, and Emlyn made some response and I heard them laughing. And suddenly, continuing the early spell of moroseness, I wanted to get away from the place, sign on a ship and sail away, resume the wandering life.

'Anchors aweigh!' Emlyn called, 'and stand by your beds! The ancient mariner is on his way!' And Amos Ellyott came stumping over the dune, a skeletal black spider against the clear blue of the sky.

I spent the afternoon avoiding him, refusing to be drawn into any more theories and speculation. 'He's a pain in the backside,' I said to Ceri as we walked along the water's edge, our long shadows ahead of us from the evening sun. We picked up shells and examined a dead starfish, and talked. I heard about the girls in London, and nights out at the concerts, and the Professor who was admired and feared. We giggled at our scalloped feet under water. We tried to make out the names of the waiting ships, guessed at their nationality. Was I musical? Only after four pints. She hadn't got it, either – not really – and would probably end up giving piano lessons in a front room. The sun was going down red, the tide coming in. Beyond the roofs of the town the bald hills were as clear as if you had a telescope to your eye. Did I remember Emlyn Morton playing the trumpet during that school assembly? Now I did, but I didn't want to talk about the past. It was here and now with me, marvelling at here and now and being with this one.

We found a hollow in the dune and sat there. I took off my jacket and spread it out on the cooling sand, and she lay back and I kissed her on the mouth, on the warm soft skin along her neck and down her shoulder. For a time like that, pausing to smile, my knee between her legs, her arms around me. Then she eased me away, brought her hand to my mouth.

'Half a ton of lipstick,' she said. And she kept her hand there and said, 'How much do you know about me, then? You don't ask questions. I'm what – a year younger than you, and I've just done one year in London.' I felt her shiver as she spoke. 'What about the gap – from leaving school to last October?' She smiled and looked up at the sky and I held her and waited. 'Haven't you heard talk about me? I had a wild time. Went off with a bloke. I was with him ten months, three weeks and a day.' She looked at me. 'Then he went back to his wife.' She took her hand away. 'Did you know?' I shook my head. 'Not here in the town –

up in the port. Mam and Dad's security must have been first class. I just thought I'd let you know.'

I tried a laugh, heard myself say, 'so what – it's your affair.' And I pulled her closer.

'I thought I'd tell you,' she said.

'Before somebody lets me know?'

She shook her head decisively, her mouth small and tight for a moment. 'No – just to tell you I'm playing around, Philip. That's how it is. Playing the field.' And she ran her hand down my side and over my thigh, rubbing between my legs. I was on top of her my mouth against hers, my knees pushing her legs apart and I was back to playing around wasn't I? Then I looked up and the marram grass above us had parted in two places, two narrow white faces there, wide eyed and watching. Robert Owen. Captain X.

I rolled over on my knees and Ceri was pulling her dress down. 'Oh, good God no,' I yelled at them. 'Will you bloody well clear off?'

'Wasn't watching,' Captain X replied, his villain's eyes fixed and unblinking.

'Just get lost, the two of you!'

'You told us off last time,' Robert Owen said, a note of hurt in his voice. 'This time, it's the truth.'

They both stood, both of them pointing up the beach in the direction of the town. I got to my feet. Ceri grabbed my arm and pulled herself up. The light wasn't good, but most of the men in a half circle at the water's edge were clearly policemen, and there was an ambulance lurching up the beach to the promenade.

'We can tell the truth when we want to, see?' Robert Owen said.

'She came in with the tide – in a boat,' Captain X

added. 'Another one of them...'

We began to walk towards the town, the boys following. Robert Owen said, 'There was a seagull sitting on her head.' It was Tom Hughes's boat, we were told, and Tom had been on the look out for it all day.

'Say you're sorry,' Robert Owen called after us.

I turned to look at them. They looked small, standing there, and very defiant. 'Why should I be sorry?'

'Liars you called us. We can tell the truth good as anybody when we want.'

'OK – sorry. Now come on with us off this beach.'

They walked between us. We saw a stretcher go into the ambulance, saw the police heave the boat up clear of the high waterline, saw the ambulance go bumping up the beach.

Captain X turned out to be a Cyril. His mother came out of the crowd on the promenade screaming, 'Come here Cyril, you bloody idiot! Murder you I will!' The town, she told us, wasn't a proper place for bringing up children any more.

Voices from the crowd told us the deceased was a widowed lady. Mrs Hilda Palmerstone. From Bristol way. Lived in a flat on the front past Ocean View. Very refined. Been in the town for most of the war. And she had gone out on the ebb tide during the night, had been there in the estuary all day long, made a landing not so very far from where Tom Hughes usually had his boat beached. Mrs Palmerstone. The fourth.

Ceri said she wanted to go home, and although she linked her arm in mine we were silent all the way. At her door she said, 'Anything I'm likely to say is going to be a waste of time. Right?' The light came on in the street. A ship in the estuary brayed across the town. I wanted to stay with her, oh Christ I wanted to talk to her, hear her talk. But I knew it would be a waste too, and I let her go. After the door had closed the street was a stony, desert place, dark and empty.

Any night but Sunday night I would have made for the first pub. But Sunday was dry-day and I wasn't a member of the only club with a seven-day license, so I headed for the Crescent, and Emlyn was up in his room at the top of the house, letting the neighbours have it with 'My Very Good Friend The Milkman', full trumpet blast. I didn't give him a knock. Anything I might say to him would be a waste of time too, I felt.

So I wandered the town – back home to Laura was unthinkable – and by the entrance to the station I paused to light a cigarette and discovered my lighter had gone. It wasn't a particularly good lighter, had one of those flames that blacken your fag. But it had come back with me from Burma and I went in search of it, remembering that I had taken my jacket off and spread it out on the sand. On the promenade, a crowd of people still there under the street lamp talking and staring out at the estuary. I kept away from them and took the steps down on to the black beach and headed for the dune. Not a chance, of course, but I had to do something for God's sake.

Your eyes become accustomed to the dark, as the story books say. I kept close to the dune, the sand I kicked up cold as ice under my trouser legs. Two stars in the sky, winking lights from the ships out in the estuary, and an occasional blast from the sirens, the lap of small waves further down the beach. Some night bird went whirring past, made me catch my breath. I tried to gauge where the hollow was, looked out to sea remembering that there had been a big tanker close inshore. A steep bank of sand that I remembered. Then a ridge of marram grass. I heard myself breathing heavily. And I was kneeling in the hollow, one hand sweeping across the cold sand. This hollow? This place? It all depends on what you remember, and what you remember of it: one of Amos Ellyott's remarks in my head. My hand closed around the lighter and I gripped it tight, and stayed there like that, and remembered her, how she looked, what she said, taste, touch...

Then there was a scuffling sound in the darkness above me. 'Who's there?' I said, and all I could think to do was flick the wheel on the lighter. It fired first time and I held it out at arm's length, staring over and beyond its ragged flame. A man there, big and bulky, crouching in the grass. His face turned slowly towards the light. 'Where am I?' Mash said.

I went over to him saying, 'It's Philip – what are you doing here?' The lighter went out, failed to fire again. 'Mash – what the hell are you doing here?' I touched his hand. Colder than the sand. 'Come on, mate – what are you doing here?'

'I was sleeping,' he said. 'I was going and I got lost.'

I put my hand under his elbow. 'Come on. You can't stay here.' He shook it away and I was suddenly afraid of him, and began talking, saying the first thing that came into my head. 'Come on. It's bloody cold – you'll get piles worse than Emlyn.'

'Emlyn?' He said. He got to his feet. 'Where's Emlyn, then?'

'In his bed,' I said. 'Come on. It's me – Philip. Let's get you home…' Then he was walking next to me along the beach, rubbing his huge hands and mumbling, 'Cold, cold, it's cold.' And I was having to stretch out to keep up with him. He was making for the lights on the promenade, but I edged him over and said 'We'll stay on the beach,' and wondered why I'd said it.

He didn't object. 'All right on the beach, Philip. Cold. I'm cold.' We both stumbled in the ruts the ambulance had made. There were still people under the same lamp on the promenade. I moved him down almost to the water's edge as we drew level with them. Rationalised the act by asking myself what I would I say to them if they asked where we'd been. Taking it no further than that, but wondering at myself all the same.

We walked on. No one yelled from the promenade, no policeman rose out of the sand to halt us. We climbed over the railings at the far end of the promenade, and now he knew where he was and went on ahead of me. I followed him to the gates of the Grange. He sprinted up the driveway without a word. The house was in darkness but lights came on all over as soon as he opened the front door. I waited for a while; I didn't know what for. Then I walked slowly back to the town.

As I went past the Crescent I could hear Emlyn still blowing away. Twice I was pulled up by the police and allowed to go after a few questions and a flash of a torch in my face. When I reached the house and searched for my key I found I had the lighter clenched tight in the palm of my hand.

A bad night. Dreams. Ceri in them, running down dark streets ahead of me. Mash at the gate of the back yard with vipers in his hands.

Monday, a morning close and sticky, thunder in the air. Laura had a bad headache, in a depression brought on by more murders, nobody safe any more, nothing certain, like the weather. She was bitten by the cleaning bug, this old house she moaned, this old town, that old shop, these terrible murders. Where was it all going to end? Mrs Palmerstone now. Beyond joking now. Nobody safe any more. People had had enough. Time the whole town joined together and put a stop to it. Hadn't everybody suffered enough in the war? All that killing. And look at us now – was it any better now what with everything still on rations and clothing coupons? There were lights in the street, but that didn't stop these terrible things going on did it? 'They teached people how to kill,' she said, looking away from me as she did so.... Laura voicing the unease and anger and suspicions of Maelgwyn town. An outrage going on. And I was connected – not responsible of course – but linked to it in Laura's and the town's mind.

'I'll go and tidy up the shop,' I said, and retreated. I had the feeling that if I had said I was going back to India she wouldn't have minded.

The shop, of course, was long since past any return to order, the stock thick as weeds in a deserted garden. I flung books about, made piles of them, swept shelves clear and stuck the same worthy volumes back again. Only a great burning would bring order. But I worked myself into a sweat, breaking off only when the traders of the Market Hall came for a chat. Mollie Ann with an apple, Nell Crockery with a dirty joke that was old when I was young, Isaac Moss Cobblers who picked nails out of his mouth as he talked. The murders, naturally. I remembered that old lift, didn't I? Well, nobody's heard it, not for years, during the day. Only at night, see. Eyes narrowed, lips pulled in. This Mrs Palmerstone took size five shoes. The birds had been at her. But it was the same man who did it – and the police knew him, could lay their hands on him any time, only there had to be evidence, see.

Without exception they ended with the same remark, followed it with an enquiring look that underlined my involvement. I wasn't a suspect, of course. I was J. Palmer Roberts's son. They had known me since I was knee high to a grasshopper... but they left statements on the air – 'fancy pushing her out in Tom's boat after' – and watched me keenly through narrowed eyes, as if they knew I could, if I wanted, come up with the answers.

'What he does,' Nell Crockery explained after giving her breasts a heave, 'is kill quick. With this strap, see. Then he plonks them somewhere else. And there's no marks on him because he's naked – no hairs or anything like that.' Her voice became spitty with relish. 'That comes from official sources – top secret as they used to say in the war.'

It was a relief to go back to the books. I had offered no explanations or theories, and that probably made me a more doubtful character than ever. What should I have said? Find Ridetski, I was certain. Alive or dead.

Shortly before Laura arrived to take over I found an old, ink-stained copy of *Tales from Shakespeare*. It had the County School stamp all over it, a real old veteran of many a classroom battle. Inside the front cover there was a string of names. The last one was Ellen Lewis,

1924. I squatted on a pile of books and lit a cigarette.

It was the entry for September 1908 that set the bells ringing. Edward Mortimer, in a rounded, child's handwriting. A name that spelled clashing swords and acts of valour. It recurred on page after page, sometimes as the Honourable Edward Mortimer, sometimes as Sir Edward Mortimer, once as Edward Mortimer, Gent. And on the inside of the back cover five lines that brought me back to Marshall Edmunds once again:

> Who's left to love?
> Only he who rages –
> Gone to ashes all the ages.
> Summer has a fine warm face,
> Winter such a cold embrace.
>
> Signed, Edward Mortimer, Poet.
> Glanmorfa House
> Maelgwyn–on–Sea,
> Wales,
> Great Britain
> The World.

I pocketed the book if only to prove to Emlyn that Edward Mortimer, Sir and Honourable and Gent and Poet, hadn't been at school in our time, and that Mash was misquoting the last line.

The house in the Crescent was silent, seemingly deserted. It always looked like that – as if the owners had done a flit and weren't expected back. But the front door was wide open, held against the wall by an empty milk bottle. I tapped on the glass of the porch door and went in calling Emlyn. My voice spiralled upwards and died. The kitchen door was open. I heard sounds of retching from the back and went down the passage calling 'Mr Morton – are you all right?'

Hot as a boiler house in the kitchen, the remains of a meal on the table. What a day to have the fire banked up. There was a large brown paper envelope on it, edges curling in the smoke. The toilet in the yard flushed and Idwal came in. He was unsteady on his legs, his face drawn and shiny with sweat, white froth at the corners of his mouth, red on his chin. He saw me and turned quickly and I knew he was replacing his teeth, then he slumped on a chair at the table. It was blood on his chin.

'Never heard you come in,' he said. Then 'Philip...' – as if he had forgotten my name.

'I'll get you a drink of water...'

'Perish the thought.' He smiled. 'A bit of morning sickness.' The blood on his chin fascinated me. I wanted to wipe it off for him. 'Must have been the heat...'

'I'll open a window.'

He shook a hand at me. 'No, no. I might catch pneumonia... My God, I could catch anything.'

I could smell sick from him. 'D'you want me to get a doctor or something?'

He forced another smile. 'No, no. It was just those bloody powdered eggs we had. In the piping days of peace, Philip – and still powdered eggs! A fag would be useful.' I held one out to him and flicked my lighter. He inhaled deeply and sat back in the chair. 'That's better. Keep up the level of the poison.' His hands were trembling. 'Life savers these – can't have doctors, Philip – they'd make me give them up!'

'I'll make you a cup of tea.'

'Philip – don't fuss. You don't have to stay. I'm all right. Emlyn's over at the boat.' There's blood on your chin, I wanted to tell him. 'Look – just one thing you can do for me. Just keep it to yourself, OK? Emlyn – such a bloody hypochondriac. He was moaning about his indigestion last night. Just – well – don't tell him.' Then he brought out his army officer's voice, like his son a good mimic. 'I must absolutely insist, Roberts, actually. Mum's the jolly old word, what?'

'Fair enough,' I said. We smiled at each other. The colour returning to his cheeks now.

'You're a good chap. Emlyn always said you were. When he was little he used to copy you.'

'Poor sod! I'll have to be going...'

'What's the reading matter in your pocket? Can I have a look?'

I gave him the book and he laid it flat on the table so that he could hide the trembling in his hands. A crooked vein throbbed in his forehead. 'Found it in the shop this morning.' He was examining the names at the front. 'There's a bit of a poem in the back. Mash is always quoting it.' He turned the pages over slowly. He was a long time reading the poem. Behind him the fire hissed in the grate.

'Philip,' he said at last, 'I don't think Marshall killed these women. Do you?'

'Well, good God, of course he didn't!'

He was still staring at the poem as he spoke. 'It's what they're saying. The consensus of opinion. Get the brain doctors in. Break him down. Philip...' it was an effort for him to say it. 'You don't think Marshall's insane, do you?'

'To hell with that,' I said firmly. 'He's... Well, not right, but he's not a loony.'

'I had a row with Emlyn about it.' He was staring at me now. 'Didn't mean to – but it came to that.' I could sense the power in him still. A hell of a man, this one – wild and daring so they said. And there was some of it left, even now. 'But – he's violent, Philip. In some kind of blackout, maybe?'

'Four blackouts?' He nodded. 'Pointless – you've got to have a motive. What about this Ridetski?'

'Yes, pointless. Most things are pointless, aren't they? In the long run.' He closed the book. 'Andy Ridetski? The cops asked me about Andy. I sold him a camera once. Very artistic bloke. Very highly strung. Bit of a crook.' He was calm again now, back to bantering. 'What a bloody situation. Ridetski come back – is that what old Mr Ellyott thinks? Oh – I have my doubts.' He flipped open the cover of the book. 'Mind if I have a read of this? Might not be too late to learn something. Improve my mind. But – well, if you want it for something it's all right.' He pushed the book along the table towards me.

'You keep it,' I said. 'What about Ridetski, though?'

He picked up the book and held it against his chest. 'I'll be sure to let you have it back – give it to Emlyn, OK?' I nodded. 'Ridetski? Well, the last time I knew him he was scared of his own shadow. Did a bunk, you know. He was running away from his missus – so why come back and kill her?'

'And he might be dead....'

Idwal Morton flashed a white smile. 'Then he'd have some difficulty in killing anybody wouldn't he?' We laughed. 'All right if I have a read of this?'

'Fine,' I said. Subject closed. I left him there in that

oven of a room. Outside, although the air was heavy and oppressive, it was, for a while, like a spring day.

As I turned a corner on to the promenade I came face to face with Amos Ellyott. 'I have been looking for you all morning,' he greeted me accusingly. 'Come quickly to my chambers.' And he turned on his heel and went stumping back to Ocean View. He was nimble that day, joints functioning, and was close to a trot on the stairs.

'You've been at the vitamins,' I told him.

'Do please refrain from witticisms,' he replied as he flung back the door. 'The first break has occurred. Come in.'

Laura wasn't the only one in the town with the tidy bug. Amos Ellyott's rooms, considering my last look at them, were neat, orderly, the books on their shelves, the bottles gone, a smell of polish on the air.

'You must come and tidy our shop,' I said.

He had the lid of a small bureau open. 'Keep your remarks to yourself,' he snapped back, then beckoned me to the desk. 'Now – tell me please – why should someone decide to send me this?' He pulled a photograph from a large envelope and placed it on a square of blotting paper. An enlargement. Ten by twelve at the least. Of a car burning in the night. Of a man with a white bag clutched to his chest, his face clearly defined in the light from the blaze. MT Edmunds. Emtee by name, but not empty by nature.

XIII

'Well?' he said. 'What do you think? Be kind enough to give me the benefit of your powers of observation.'

He was wearing a white linen jacket over a waistcoat and cardigan and he smelled strongly of mothballs and old dust. 'I'd say you had this photograph when we were messing about in that tower.'

'Not at all, not at all. Do not presume. Observe the near professionalism of our friend Ridetski. Such gloss, such clarity. Use the magnifying glass. Observe.' There were two other figures on either side of MT. Two darker shapes that had to be men. They came up clearly under the magnifying glass. Two headless men. Three men at a burning.

'Well? Well?' He growled impatiently. 'Your comments, please.'

Guess who? I thought. Had George Garston cast his photograph into a grate, as that sick man in an oven of a room had done? Idwal Morton in the back doorway, blood on his chin, trembling hands fumbling at his buttons, the brown paper curling in the smoke above the hissing fire. Three men at a burning.

'Oh – Philip!' How silently she moved. Such a big, angular heavy-footed woman. To come up the creaking staircase so lightly, make so quiet an entrance through the open door. 'I see you've got it, Mr Ellyott,' she said, and Amos and I bumped each other as we turned, and she was standing there – such a drab dress, so many wrinkles in her stockings – the broad, strong hands as if working the needles, her glasses down on her nose.

'Dear lady,' Amos said 'Mrs Edmunds – you startled me. Do please be seated.' He moved like an elderly waiter around her, first to draw up a chair, then to close the door.

Laura always referred to her as Miss Lloyd – and the name of her house – always with respect. A lady. Her father a big man in shipping. A family to be classed among the gentry, Maelgwyn being short on dukes and lords and squires. Miss Lloyd Glanmorfa House for identification. Glanmorfa House – which MT had changed to the Grange. I remembered the book and the poem. Was this Edward Mortimer, honourable and sir and gent and poet, Form 1A, September 1908? 'Who's left to love? Only he who rages...' The neat, rounded handwriting, a little girl's voice at a time of sadness... I looked at her hollowed, bony face, her sparse hair and felt as if I had solved something.

Then she spoke. 'It was I who sent you that photograph, Mr Ellyott.' A plain statement, delivered at speed: a driven woman.

'You, madam? I don't understand. Why to me? May I offer you a glass...'

'Nothing.' An emphatic shake of the head. 'I sent it to you because you are my only hope. The police are persecuting my son.' Even Amos had no immediate reply for that one. 'They questioned him for the better part of the morning. He cannot remember, Mr Ellyott. He doesn't know what they are talking about. Yesterday afternoon he had a breakdown. A nervous collapse. The doctor gave him a sedative. He slept. Then when I went up to see him in the evening he'd gone – out through the window; climbed down the drainpipe.' I stared at one of Amos's muddy pictures on the wall above her head. 'When he came back he said he was running away! He said he'd been with you, Philip.'

'That's right, Mrs Edmunds.'

She was surprised and grateful. Her face softened. 'Honestly, Philip?' She held back from touching me.

'I met him on the prom. We had a walk together on the beach...'

'But he said he was running away.' She appealed to Amos. 'That's what he said.'

'In jest, surely?'

'Jest, Mr Ellyott? We are all past jesting. Are you aware what they are doing to him? These continual questions, day in day out?' She turned to me. 'Was Emlyn with you?'

'Just the two of us. Emlyn was at home.'

'He's been very good. Both of you have. You met him on the prom, honestly?' I nodded. 'Emlyn went with him this morning to the Police Station. That Inspector Marks! Why doesn't he leave the boy alone?' She sat on the edge of the chair, both feet planted firmly on the floor, and there should have been knitting needles in her hands. 'But you boys have been through it, haven't you? Fought for your country. Fought to free the world from tyrants.' I looked at my shoes, embarrassed and surprised – Sylvia Edmunds waving the flag. 'But what was he doing? Dubious business deals with the like of George Garston. Traitor is too good a word to use.' She choked on the words and removed a handkerchief from up her sleeve and held it to her mouth.

'You say you sent me this photograph?' Amos enquired in a low voice.

'I did.' She dabbed at her upper lip. 'It came through the post. I thought it was an advert or something and I opened it.'

'Addressed to your husband? A picture of a man standing near a vehicle in flames.'

She flared up at that. 'His picture – stealing that money. Didn't I tell you he was nearly bust? Well – that is where he got the money from...'

'Did you show it – to Mr Edmunds?'

She got to her feet and shook her head. 'For some more fancy stories? More lies? The truth has got to come out. From the beginning...'

'Then – can you suggest who might have sent you this photograph?'

'They were all in on it,' she said flatly. 'A terrible war for our survival going on and they were thieving. Probably the least of their crimes. He's afraid of it coming out. Of course he is. Prepared to sacrifice anybody to save his own skin. I've got my boy to protect.'

'George Garston, perhaps?' Amos suggested.

'I am not prepared to speculate, Mr Ellyott. But – you've got to begin there. With that picture.' In a couple of long, smooth strides she was at the door. 'I sent it to you because you have the expertise in these matters. I have no faith whatsoever in the police.' She pulled the door open.

'Madam, please,' Amos appealed to her.

'What I am telling you is the truth. You start there. With that picture.' She turned to face us. 'That is what is being covered up. Good morning to you. Good morning, Philip.' She went out, closed the door softly, and there wasn't a sound as she descended the stairs.

I went to the window. She had a car out there. I heard it start, a grind of gears as it pulled away but I couldn't see it. Across the road, on the promenade, leaning against the railings, MT alone, staring out at the grey ships in the estuary.

'Let us write down a few names, metaphorically speaking,' Amos said. 'Let us write down Mr MT Edmunds. Let us write Mr George Garston. Let us write...' And he came up close and stared at me over his glasses, made his cigarette flip against his nose. 'Let us write Mr Idwal Morton.'

'Oh, bollocks,' I said.

He cackled at me. 'It depends on what you're looking for, Philip. Truth is a dreadfully distasteful dish. Let us add another name. Mrs Sylvia Edmunds. Don't make that dreadful, uncouth remark. I saw you shiver as she went out. Doesn't she move quickly, silent as an animal? What lady would suspect another at the dead of night? A lady soured and desperate, ready to do anything to protect her offspring. A lady stunted by so much bitterness...'

'You're out of your mind. Mrs Edmunds? Knocking off all these old women? Good God – you might as well put me on your list, metaphorically speaking.'

He went *tk*, *tk*, *tk*. 'You are on it already. You and Emlyn Morton and Marshall Edmunds. But set that aside..."

'Thank you very much.'

'Let us consider this extraordinary visit.' I went over to the window. Ceri Price rode past on the promenade, skirt riding high over brown legs, her dog in the bicycle basket. She looked great, and oh God, playing the field. My breath caught in my throat. 'Philip,' came the nagging old voice behind me. 'The picture is important not because of what it says but because of what it implies. The first murder is the one – she fits, Philip, she fits. The others are a blind. A false trail.' I laughed at him and he trembled with rage. 'Why should she kill Mrs Ridetski you ask? For Marshall's sake – that's why. The lady's out for vengeance. She has been wronged.'

'Oh, balls, balls, balls,' I said.

We were silent for a long time after that. Ever since Mrs Edmunds had gone we'd been arguing, and I realised suddenly that I didn't want this old man to come up with a solution, and that was why I stayed while the sun broke through outside and the day brightened. I wanted a solution, of course I did, but it had to be acceptable.

'What about Ridetski?' I started up again. 'If he isn't in that Tower then why can't he be knocking around the town wearing a beard, or something?'

'A possibility,' he conceded. 'Ridetski holds everything together, doesn't he? You have come round to it at last...'

'Now – just a minute – it was all Mrs Edmunds...'

He rose stiffly from his chair and came to join me at the window. 'Philip – I will come clean, as they say. In a game of cards you offer one sometimes in order to make your opponent commit himself...'

'Do you, really? I never knew that.'

He grated his teeth and made his ticking noise, but controlled himself sufficiently to say, 'It was I who sent Mrs Edmunds a photograph!'

'You did? Where the hell did you get if from?' Then I was pointing at him, saying, 'It was you who stripped the wallpaper in Lilian's place, wasn't it?'

'It was never orthodox,' he said defensively. 'I must insist on your total discretion.'

'You bloody old burglar! You've been keeping them from the police, haven't you? Withholding evidence.'

But he came back fighting. 'And I had every right! After that boy scout Inspector ordered me off. Every right in the world.' Old fox, I thought. No wonder the bloody police weren't making any progress. 'This may be Ellyott's last case,' he added, placing his hand on his heart to see if it was still pumping.

'Don't give me that! You found that picture, didn't you? And you sent it to her in the post?'

'No, no, no. You must not anticipate. Do not presume. I did not send her that photograph.'

Senile decay, I thought. 'Look – you just told me...'

'I sent her another photograph – and she sent me this one in return.'

I gaped at him, which was what he had wanted me to do all along. 'So she's got some pictures, too?'

He eased his glasses a little further down his nose. 'Mrs Ridetski's rooms, you will remember, were broken into and left in some disorder on the night she died...'

'Mrs Edmunds?'

'Why not? The night of Mrs Ridetski's death – might Mrs Edmunds not have gone there to talk, to persuade, to beg perhaps that the association with Marshall end? And might she not have found a door ajar, Mrs Ridetski having left in a hurry to keep a fatal appointment?' He made his ticking noises, his sharp, youthful eyes on me all the time. 'Mrs E goes up the stairs. Might she not have found the photograph in some drawer perhaps? A photograph like that one and its variations – other faces in view, perhaps? Stretching coincidence to its limits, might not Mrs Ridetski have been inspecting the photographs that evening, in preparation for a little blackmail herself? Who knows? Mrs E, we now know, took the photographs, searched for more and failed to find any. Home she went – and may well have sent them out appropriately.' He did his grating laugh then. 'Your face, Philip. My word, what naive young men came off the battlefields!'

'You're just supposing. Somebody else might have sent her the photo – and why should she want to send them out, anyway?' I could hear the fire hissing in that kitchen in the Crescent, see the brown paper envelope curling in the heat.

'What young men you are. So much experience to so little effect. Do you remember the wreath in the Tower?'

'What's that got to do with it?'

'What did it say? "To a brave warrior"?'

'Something like that. What's a wreath got to do with it? We were talking about photographs.'

'Would you care to look closer?' He went over to the bureau and took the photograph out. 'Come,' he said, 'come closer. You can't possibly examine it from that distance.' I went over to him. 'Observe. The photograph which the lady has admitted sending to me. Now – are you observing – the quality of the picture? The technique is called montage – but the head rests uneasily on the shoulders, surely? Not quite in place?' His finger pointed urgently. 'What do you say? *Tk, tk, tk.*'

‘A fake?’

‘A not entirely successful first attempt, I deduce. Mr Ridetski at the bonfire clicked his camera, but the results were short on clarity. Help was required. A little montage in the dark room. Our friend Ridetski would not have used this one. No – I am prepared to wager that his skill improved, and that he threatened our friends with more accomplished versions; Mr MT’s head on this one, Messrs Garston and Morton on the others. Three men at a bonfire, each clutching a bag of gold. The lady decided it was time for me to see it.’ His mottled hand trembled as he opened a small drawer in the bureau and removed another photograph, no more than postcard size, blank side uppermost. ‘Now – so that you may have a complete picture! This is the one I sent to the lady, the card I preferred. I had copies made.’ He looked up at me, then examined the photograph, hiding it from me before he handed it over. ‘How long ago, Philip? Five years? Six? Perhaps more?’

It was a sunny day. Perhaps they were out on bikes, the edge of a wheel on the grass by her leg. And the way I saw it he had a camera on a tripod and he had set the time exposure and had run back to her before the shutter opened... A tall, slim man, dark and with a thin, sensitive face. In Royal Air Force uniform, with Poland above his badge of rank. And she had removed her glasses, and the wind had swept back her hair, a blouse open at her throat, and she was looking up at him, as pretty as she would ever be, perhaps as happy. Sylvia Edmunds for sure. Andrei Ridetski it had to be.

We walked to the King’s Arms for a beer, and the voices were saying fog, bound to be that old fog after a morning so humid broken by such a burning sun. If not tonight then tomorrow – one of them bloody fogs. I found myself listening intently, concentrating on a conversation endlessly repetitive to save myself from thinking about Sylvia Edmunds. Now and then the old man, planted on a stool, his hands on the silver knob of his stick, his chin on his hands, looked at me expectantly, as if waiting for a comment or a word of congratulation. But I said nothing. I should have left him, gone home to the cold meat Laura left on Mondays, but I wanted to be near him and couldn't explain why... The fog; bound to cop it. I felt as if it was out there, at the mouth of the estuary, waiting.

'You should ask what happens next,' he said. 'I'll tell you.' Preening himself, an old cockerel perched on that stick. 'It's breaking now; beginning to move. Some more pressure may be necessary but she's an intelligent woman. It shouldn't take her long to realise it was I who sent her the photograph.'

Sylvia Edmunds in her tall, wickerwork chair, needles stabbing in her hands. A wreath for Ridetski. Had there been one for every year? Hopeful crows flying off with them? I looked around the bar, saw it reflected in a funfair mirror, all faces distorted and talking about fog. 'I'm going,' I said to him. They were dying to get off the fog and on to us, anyway.

'Wait, wait, I'll come with you!' Like a child calling after me, kicking his feet like one because he was stuck, joints locked. The regulars stared at us as I went back to straighten him, stand by until his circulation was restored. 'Thought I was doomed to listen to this conversation for ever,' he announced loudly as we went out.

Once we were outside he kept on saying – 'you must be careful what you tell Marshall – his mind clears, you know.'

'Good God! You don't think I'd tell Mash, do you?'

We headed for the promenade, bickering as we went. Ceri Price went waving by on a bicycle. Oh God, problems everywhere.

'All right,' I said savagely, 'you tell Emlyn – but neither you nor Emlyn's going to say a word to Mash. Because you're bloody wrong about Mrs Edmunds. There's nothing to connect her with any murder.'

'The unthinkable, Philip? You are Welsh. Emotion obscures logic. There is a background here, that's all I am saying. Old affairs, old intrigues...'

'Oh, come on,' I said, 'my feet are boiling.'

The sand on the dune was on fire. I waited for him and gave him my arm. I shouldn't be here, I thought, struggling up burning sand with this old fox, my shirt sticking to my back. I should be chasing after Ceri, and to hell with the endless problems he posed. 'You wouldn't leave me to die in this desert, would you?' He said. 'A loyal young man like you.'

'Just don't give me ideas,' I said.

Before we came in sight of the *Ariadne* we heard Emlyn's trumpet, the thump of a bass drum, and I knew that they had let Mash go. We stood panting at the top of the last rise on the dune. Emlyn was giving out with the Saints, marching around the boat, Captain X and Robert Owen and Sian Thomas in line behind him, with Mash at the rear, the drum on his chest.

'I can walk by myself,' Amos said, shrugging my arm away, and he trotted down, waving his stick and calling to them. I couldn't help thinking that people approached Emlyn always with pleasure. Well, this old man had news to dampen any party.

Emlyn Morton had a natural politeness. He fussed around Amos and set aside a chair for him on the deck. 'Wants to talk to me alone,' he said, rolling his eyes. 'Go and help Mash catch tiddlers for the kids.' The children, Mash too, were speckled with mud after stamping around the boat, but there was scarcely a spot on Emlyn, and he wasn't even sweating.

I peeled off my shirt, took my shoes and socks off and rolled my trousers up.

'Aren't your legs brown?' Sian Thomas said admiringly. Mash was sweeping the muddy water with a net on a pole, and giving it his full concentration.

'Hullo, Philip,' he said, and I remembered as a boy feeling intimidated by his size, felt it now, too. But the children were chattering at me and so there I was knee deep in the river, flexing my toes in the soft mud, searching for flatfish.

'Got one!' Mash cried out, and he carefully removed a shrimp from the net and dropped it in Robert Owen's jam jar. 'Coppers asking me questions all the morning,' he said. 'How many fish we got now?' I could see the thin line of the scar under his hair.

Captain X came close to say, 'Call me Captain X remember. Tell anybody it's Cyril and I'll kill you!' Robert Owen said, 'We saw you with that lady.' A ventriloquist's face, not a tremor from the lips. Down here, near the old boat, a kind of different world. But on deck the old man was still talking to Emlyn. 'Copped another!' Mash called out, and we all gathered around him to look.

‘Flying blind,’ Emlyn whispered his verdict. ‘Upside down in a cloud, poor old sod.’ Amos was asleep on the chair, his chin down on his chest, gold spectacles dangling free of his inflamed nose. ‘You’d expect that, wouldn’t you? The old blood not pumping to the brain like it should? Mrs MT! Well – I mean to say, we’ve always known she’s a bit grim, but she’s not that fucking grim, is she? You saw some pictures, honestly?’

‘A couple.’ I described them to him.

He frowned deeply. ‘I never heard anything about her and Ridetski. I mean, I used to have a fair amount of short visits back here, and there was nobody chatting about it then. Mind you – there was a blackout, and all sorts of sporting activities went on in that.’ Emlyn with his smooth, boyish face, rounded and unmarked. The full mouth smiling, dismissing Amos’s great theories so lightly. ‘Look, what he’s doing, the old boy here, is making a real story about it all. Every time he comes out with something it’s got PLOT written all over it. Remember the description of the car full of money crashing into that field? And he wasn’t even there! Now on the strength of one snapshot he’s got Mrs MT dropping her knickers for Ridetski! Big affair going on. Well – I ask you. Out of character, isn’t it? And it all comes back to character in the end. What are you starting at?’

‘You,’ I said. ‘You’re a bloody genius.’

‘Please,’ he said, eyes closed, ‘Not too much praise. It’s a hot day and my brain cells get all excited.’

‘Just tell me who’s got the character, then.’

He looked straight at me. ‘Not MT for a start. I mean, he’s all wind and piss, isn’t he? But George Garston could do it. He’s deep, old Garston.’ The old man grunted in his sleep and Emlyn drew closer, his knees pulled up under his chin. His hair was going, thinning all over the crown like Idwal's. 'My old boy could do it, too,' he added lightly. 'Idwal the Great...'

I felt my breath catch in my throat. He'd always had this way of coming out with something that caught you unawares. Saying the unsayable.

'Why not? You see, I'm a natural coward – OK? I mean, I'm really shit scared. No kidding. But Idwal's got the guts. Enough for the two of us. And he was more than likely mixed up in all the business with the money from that car. Oh God, yes. The only trouble with Idwal is he boozed it all away. Booze and bints...'

'Not your old man, Emlyn – Jesus...'

'Well of course he was mixed up in it. Any old racket.'

'But he wouldn't start knocking anybody off, would he?'

He pressed his mouth between his knees and blew his cheeks out. 'Well – you asked for suspects and I was going through the list. Idwal's got cancer, anyway.'

And that rocked me, too. I had to look around, reach for the fags. I didn't know what to say.

'It's in the stomach.' The same direct statement. 'I got him to the quack two weeks ago. It's no joy, I think.' He blew into his knees again. 'Old Amos Ellyott says everything starts with a stolen payroll and a car on fire – and you can bet your boots Idwal would be in on that. Our old house was in the bank. He was flat broke. Skint. You'll be looking at a picture of him next...'

'Oh, hell – I'm sorry, Emlyn...'

'That's how it is.' His mouth was tight and unsmiling. 'Tough for him. Got a fag?' I handed him one. 'All right

– he was in that business with MT and George Garston. No doubt about that. But – you can't very well trot up to him and say, "Father, you haven't by any chance been knocking off these women, have you?"' He inhaled a lungful. 'I mean to say. But – he could do it, old Idwal. He could do anything, that man. Nothing would surprise me. One time when I came home on leave – it was the first train in the morning. Pitch dark. I'd been travelling all the way from some bloody horrible place in Holland. Practically dead on arrival, I was. There was nobody on the platform, not even the guard. Then he comes out of the steam: Idwal the great. Nobody else. Just me and Idwal. And he comes up to me and he puts his arms around me, and he kisses me... actually kisses me...' His eyes were bright and shining. Once more a great gulp of smoke. 'Look Philip – let's just keep Idwal's state of health to ourselves, OK? Don't tell Sherlock here, I mean – and for Christ's sake don't tell him anything else, either! He's got it all cocked up as it is.' He got to his feet and brushed down his flannels. 'I think I'll stretch my legs...'

'Stop splashing me!' Sian Thomas wailed from below.

'We were having a great time, weren't we? You and me celebrating life – in the happy ever after time, before everything went shitty. All those coppers chasing Mash. One of them's been up there on the dunes all afternoon – did you see him? Maybe I shouldn't have told that Inspector to go and kiss his arse this morning.' He smiled down at me. 'I was ever so polite about it, mind.'

'I bet,' I managed to say.

He stared solemnly at Amos. 'I think he's got himself all tangled up with a car on fire and a vanishing payroll. Didn't contradict him, mind. It'll be someone connected with Lilian...'

'Ridetski?'

'Not a bad bet,' he agreed. 'Did you know the coppers have been interviewing some of the most respectable business men in town? Did you know they keep on calling Davy Garston in? Old Lilian – she had such a hell of a lot of visitors. No disrespect, but I dropped a real bollock when I got us going on that, didn't I? Know what I want? A bit of ordinary living. I've told Percy Davies I'll come into the office next Monday.' He slapped his thigh. 'I'll take a stroll. You put the kettle on for tea. We'll send old Mash up there with a cup for the Gestapo, OK?'

Then Amos awoke. 'Boys – I'm bursting!' He tried to get up. 'And I'm stuck! Quickly now – quickly! Give a hand. Oh hasten, hasten!'

We grabbed an elbow each and carried him, bent as he was to the side of the boat. 'I'll just test the wind,' Emlyn said, dabbing a finger against his tongue and holding it up.

'Straighten me!' the old man roared. Mash and the children stepped out from under the boat to watch. We tottered there as we pushed his knees down. 'Hurry! Please! Hurry!'

'All right – fire!' Emlyn told him. 'Come on – I'm not getting it out for you!' Amos fumbled with his buttons. 'What's the matter – has it disappeared? Sian Thomas – close your eyes!' We were just in time too. The old man shuddered and made ecstatic noises, and we held him there and bit back great gulps of laughter. Robert Owen and Captain X were so overcome they had to sit on the mud. Sian Thomas watched, wide eyed and with clinical detachment. She was holding Mash's hand, and was spattered with mud.

'I don't think I need that walk now,' Emlyn said.

Afterwards we made tea, then Emlyn brought out his trumpet and played great, swinging versions of Welsh hymns that set the children jiving. He kept it going on the down slopes of the dunes too, until we reached the promenade where MT was waiting with a car to take Mash home. MT didn't have much to say for himself, seemed preoccupied, and he drew away quickly with Amos Elloytt waving to us from the front seat.

'Mash is under doctor's orders,' Emlyn explained. 'By the way – I won't be around tonight, either. Got me a date. I'm taking Ceri Price to the pictures.' Then he looked at me. 'You don't mind, do you?'

'Press on regardless,' I said, and cursed myself for minding, and walked home kicking at loose chippings on the pavement, talking to myself. Well, she had told me she was playing around, hadn't she?

I came face to face with Will Wilkins at the gate. He was wearing a blue apron under his coat and was heading back to his shop to cash up and sweep out. 'Philip,' he said, 'just the man I wanted to see!' His face was the texture of sweaty dough. I guessed he'd been chasing Laura around the kitchen again. He whipped a handkerchief from up his sleeve, held it under his nose and spoke through it. 'Would it be convenient for me to ask for your stepmother's hand in marriage?' My day for surprises. I shouldn't have laughed.

XIV

I decided on the George, a pub I usually avoided, for what looked like being a solitary Monday night. On the way there I saw Emlyn and Ceri moving with the queue into the Regal, and I never tasted the first pint, found myself chain-smoking, hating everybody. Especially the barmaid, in her apron, looking like she was made of starched white linen, dispensing the drinks, her thin nose registering disapproval at the speed at which I had emptied my glass. In the George you took your beer in sips, and watched the door furtively, and kept the windows shut in case the fresh air ruined the smell of disinfectant. There were warnings everywhere about spitting, gambling and singing being forbidden. But it was either the George or the Anchorage, and I felt safer from Amos here where beer was sinful, conversation mumbling about death.

But I was wrong, of course. At half past eight he prodded the door open with his stick and came stumbling in. 'Philip,' he bellowed. 'My God!'

'No swearing if you please,' the barmaid screeched in protest.

'What the hell are you doing here, Philip?' He went on, each word like a stabbing lance. 'This place! Good God Almighty!'

'Any more swearing and I send for the police!' The barmaid warned him, and I was glad she'd said it because he now gave her his undivided attention.

He propped his stick against the counter and planted his elbows on the bar and brought his hands together in a sharp crack that made her jump. 'I am the police,' he announced. 'Have you ever been prosecuted for the supplying of despair, madam?'

'I keep an orderly house. We don't have no trouble here!'

'You don't keep anything here,' Amos told her. 'One neat gin and a beer for my colleague – poor, deluded boy who thought he could hide from me – and you have my permission to risk a fragrant smile.'

But she was a tough old bird. 'You've had enough. No drinks for you here. I've got the right, see. I know the law.' She brought her thin, lethal nose within inches of his. 'You clear off!' she said, spit glistening on her lower lip.

'I will not clear off!' Amos replied. 'Send for the forces, the magistrates and town clerks. I will not be ordered out while my money is on the table.'

Not bad for a Monday night slanging match, I thought. Some of the customers who had been dying over their drinks were now sitting up and seemed almost lively. The old man had obviously toured the pubs in his search for me, and he was more than three sheets to the wind. I stood back and watched and listened, not without admiration, even though it was all childish and pointless. But now I had him for the rest of the night, and Amos Ellyott sober had to be suffered; Amos Ellyott drunk was not to be tolerated. I was about to go looking for the back door when a heavy voice from the corner threatened to put him out. 'It'll have to be the two of us,' I told the room, and was appalled to realise that what I wanted this Monday night was a fight.

Fortunately the only response to my remark came from Amos. 'My dear boy,' he said, turning his back on the barmaid, 'thank you for that show of loyalty.' And he held out a cold hand for me to grip. His rheumy eyes glistened. 'Had Adolf Hitler succeeded in invading this country, rest assured that this dismal excuse for a public house would be the seat of the Gestapo.'

'I think we should go to a pub, Mr Ellyott,' I suggested.

'Admirable, admirable,' he replied in a choked voice. We headed for the door.

'Good riddance to both of you!' The barmaid was for having the last word. And as the old man appeared to be too overcome with emotion, or gin, I spoke for him. 'You want to have your drains seen to. You've gassed those two in the corner.'

We went out on a flood of words from the barmaid, the old man chuckling. At the door the fog met us like a wall.

The fog was a Maelgwyn wonder, something that recurred in conversation and stories over the years. Some of them had punctuated my childhood and I had forgotten until that night how they filled the streets of the town, how dense they were. They occurred always in high summer. They lasted a few days – although I remembered my father saying that one of them, in 1896, had stayed down for a fortnight. Ten miles outside the town, a few thousand feet up in the air, the sun would be shining. They were phenomena peculiar to Maelgwyn and they were a visitation from on high of course. And a bad omen.

'Can't see a bloody thing,' Amos said.

'So stop walking up my leg,' I said. 'And look – just for one night I don't want to talk about murders and I don't want any more theories – all right?'

'I am no longer at the theory stage,' he snapped back. Then he discovered that he was not wearing his glasses. We had not reached the porch of the King's Arms. 'I've got to have them. I'm blind without them. Were they on my nose in that dreadful pub?' I told him I couldn't remember if they were or not, but one thing's for sure, if we went back there it would be a lynching party. I called for drinks at the bar of the King's Arms, but he went on moaning about his glasses.

'Go back home and have a look,' I told him, 'I'll wait for you here.'

He rapped his stick against the bar. 'Would you have me expire in that filthy fog out there? Would you?' All the saloon bar sitting up, silent, and watchful. Drink your poison, I said and let's go. 'No need for you to sound so petulant,' he replied. Outside the fog had thickened. We stumbled along in the general direction of the promenade. The braying sirens from the ships in the estuary were muffled but somehow more urgent. People came up to us out of the fog, then vanished. And Amos talked. 'George Garston, the one party in this case who remains a complete puzzle. It is my belief that it was he who fired those shots when we were investigating the Tower.'

A man came out of the fog. Seeing us, he changed course, but I glimpsed the outline of his face. Idwal Morton? It was. Bareheaded, great dome of a forehead. There was no mistaking him. Sick man in the fog.

I followed Amos up the creaking staircase to his rooms. He reached for his key above the door and pushed it into the lock, and it wouldn't turn. He gave the knob a twist, the door opened and I felt the hairs rise on the back of my hands. He switched on the light. Chairs overturned. Cushions on the floor, papers from the bureau scattered everywhere, his books swept off the shelves. The door to the bedroom was wide open, mattress and blankets in an untidy heap on the floor. I looked at him, and he was smiling.

'She worked it out that it was I who sent her the photograph,' he said. Then he knelt and pushed a strip of carpet back into place. If I had one photograph, then I must have more...'

'You knew this was going to happen,' I said. 'That's why you made me come back with you.' He took his glasses from an inside pocket and waved them at me. 'You're a deceitful old sod! What have you proved, anyway? Only that she wants the pictures.'

He glared at me. 'Now I have her on the run, don't you see? Depths to Mrs Edmunds – depths so clearly absent in her husband. She is about to break. Don't be sentimental, Philip. She is quite prepared to let her spouse take the blame.' He stopped short there, as if something else had occurred to him. He was staring into the bedroom. Slowly he heaved himself to his feet. Stick pointing, he shuffled across the room to the bedroom door. A singing sound from the electric lightbulb above my head. He groped along the wall for the switch. The light came on. Fog at the window open wide. I stood behind him in the doorway. 'It's the way the mattress is lying,' he whispered, fear now in his voice. He took two strides forward and pushed at the blankets with the end of his stick. And she was there.

Her hands up as if she was holding the knitting needles. Her glasses dangling from one ear across her chin. Blood on the lenses, her skin dark as blood. There had been something tight around her long neck, something that had bitten deep into the flesh. A sound from her, a pocket of air escaping.

'Downstairs. The basement flat. Telephone.' Amos's voice across a great, echoing and empty wasteland. The broken stillness of her. I saw him search for a pulse beat in the throat. 'Phone the Inspector,' he said, 'never mind the ambulance.'

This one a different death. Not simply because she was the first victim I had seen close up, but in every way. She had been dead no more than an hour; she had been left where she had been killed; a clumsier job, someone said, more signs of a struggle; her handbag was missing; and above all she was someone the others had never been – a native of the town. When I reached home at one in the morning Laura was still up, in tears. Sylvia Edmunds. Mrs MT. Miss Lloyd that was. A somebody.

The hours between had been all coming and going, uniformed and plain clothes men moving about purposefully, a photographer's blinding flash bulb, powder for prints, specimens stored in envelopes for analysis, and I, left standing in one corner, Amos in another. Men went running through the fog to MT's house and came back with the news that Mash was in a drugged sleep, in bed all evening. It was MT they took to the police station. No, not one of the other tenants had heard anything or seen anyone, and they had all been in because of the fog... Inspector Marks was closeted with Amos for a long time, and Amos emerged, truculent and pinch-mouthed to watch a carpet raised in his living room, a floor board prised up and a large, manilla envelope handed over. 'I require statements as to how you came into possession of these photographs,' the Inspector declared. 'Now – have you any more hidden away?'

'You find Ridetski, dead or alive,' Amos replied. 'You get your men working on that Tower.' He winked at me as he followed the Inspector out, but when I helped to settle him in at a boarding house a few doors away he was in a raging temper. 'They want to know it all.' He kept on saying, 'and don't dare ask me to enter into discussion with you about it.'

These details a flickering film, out of sequence in my head, all the way home and in the kitchen over countless cups of tea with Laura, and in bed as I fought back sleep. Mr Stubbs, the office boy dashing in to say, 'Both Garstons, sir – and the Mortons – accounting for their movements now. Squad ready to move to the Tower.' A loop of film in a projector that showed no sign of stopping. Then sleep, and a boy at the door to our backyard, the snakes writhing in his hands.

White fog, dense as smoke, in the morning streets. A warm, very damp fog such as occurs in the tropics. Visibility no more than a few feet, so that you came upon buildings and people unexpectedly and found your way from memory. I made for Emlyn's house. The front door was closed and locked. No one came in response to my knocking. I tried the back door and that too was locked. No lights anywhere, no sounds, an empty house. Both of them in the police station still? Or had Emlyn gone to the Grange to see Mash? I hurried, full of unease, to the Haven Hotel where Amos Ellyott had been found a night's lodging.

'Out,' Miss Williams said. She was one of Laura's friends, a nervous woman. She kept the door half open, most of her body behind it. 'Philip – I remember when you were little. It's worse than the old war, isn't it?'

'Did he say where he was going?'

She shook her narrow head. 'He's a very strange old man,' she said. 'Do you know – he was out nearly all of the night. Never said where, though. You came, didn't you? And the police. But no sooner had you gone than he was out of the house. "If anybody wants to see me," he said, "tell them I'm in bed!" Then out he went. It was early hours when he came back.'

'Did he leave a message for me?' Once again a decisive shake of the head. I felt left out, abandoned. 'Didn't he mention anything?'

Miss Williams' eyes flickered nervously. 'What's happened in town is too much,' she said, a break in her voice. 'I don't get nice people staying here any more. All he said to me was, 'Madam – I do not wish to speak to you,' and all I asked was about his breakfast – was it all right?' She dabbed a finger first under one eye, then the other. 'Too much, too much.' I told her I'd call back later. 'Everybody's strange,' she called after me, 'Everybody's gone strange.'

There were only a few customers in the Market Hall, and they had come to talk not to buy. Even Isaac Moss Cobblers had downed tools and stood there with the traders, a hammer in his hand. Grim faces, all of them. No jokes about this one, the different death.

I kept out of their way. Let Laura tell them what I had seen. I crept into the shop and waited for her, startled her when she came, her hands fluttering at her breasts. 'Philip – you should have stopped in bed. You've had a shock. I heard you shouting in your sleep.'

'Why do you call her Miss Lloyd Penmorfa Villa?' She stared at me dumbfounded, shaking her head slowly. 'It's all right – just a thought I woke up with.'

'Poor Mrs Edmunds? Well – before she married MT she was Miss Lloyd, bless her – and her father had Penmorfa Villa.'

'No,' I said, 'no – it was Glanmorfa House. Miss Lloyd Glanmorfa House – where Mash lives now. MT changed the name.'

She laughed and touched my arm. 'Oh, Philip – you are in a pickle! It was Idwal Morton's wife Ellen who used to live in Glanmorfa House! Her family had it, remember? Belongs to rich people from Liverpool. They changed the name to Blundellsands or something.

Idwal Morton turning the pages of the *Tales from Shakespeare*. 'I left my memory in India,' I said. Idwal Morton's face in the fog.

'You go home,' she advised me. 'There's aspirins in the cupboard above the sink. You've had a shock.'

But I walked around the town in the fog. I sat over a cup of coffee in Bodawens, hoping that Ceri might come in. What the hell was I bothering my head about that poem for? 'Summer has a fine warm face'. Oh, Jesus. Edward Mortimer, Sir and Honourable, Gent and Poet. A little girl with a fountain pen in her hand. Ellen Morton, dead a long time now – I couldn't remember her maiden name – and not Miss Lloyd Penmorfa Villa. And so what? No significance there, surely? You got the houses mixed up, Philip Roberts. Drink your coffee. Come on Ceri, show up. Have another fag. Let your mind alone.

And then there was a hand on my shoulder. 'Are you Philip Roberts?' A tall, plump man, red hair in a crew cut. He looked like police to me. Heavy freckles on his face, wearing a grubby raincoat with damp patches on it, mud on his boots.

'Philip Roberts,' I agreed. There was a suggestion of freckles in his eyes. Here we go, back to the police station, I thought. Well, that was something positive, at least – and I might catch up with Emlyn and his old man there.

'Davies, CID,' he said. 'Look – you know David Garston, don't you? We're looking for him.'

'What's up – is he lost?'

'Don't be funny, mister. He's done a bunk. This bloody fog. You seen anything of him?'

'I thought you had him in.' The man sat down next to me and looked as if he was ready for a rest. 'Has he made a run for it?'

'I never said that...'

'Well – have you tried his home?' Christ, I thought, Davy Garston. And felt relieved.

'How d'you think I got all this shit on me?' He said, looking down at his boots.

'Davy Garston – you want him?'

'I don't want him. I want to get off bloody duty, mate, and get my head down.' He sighed heavily. 'You've not seen him then?'

'Not a sign,' I said. 'If I do – shall I tell him you're looking for him?'

'Very funny,' he said. 'You got funny mates as well.

That old man, that Emlyn Morton – they was out there, digging in all that cowshit.'

The news floored me. 'At Garston's farm?' He nodded. By God, I thought, and felt the blood pound in my head. Abandoned. Left out. Well of all the miserable bloody tricks to play. He'd picked Emlyn. 'What were they digging for?' I said.

He got to his feet and stretched and yawned. 'Search me. For worms? Maybe they're going fishing.'

'What about Mr Morton? Is he in the police station still?'

'Look, matey, I can't talk about who's in the station and who isn't. You've not seen this young Garston right? If you do – say nothin'. Just come and tell us, OK?' My turn to nod. He went out and I felt more alone than ever.

I left the cafe and started to wander. Lights on in the houses, only a few people out and about, blinds down on many windows. Maelgwyn a secret place, like a town occupied by the enemy. Lights in every window on St John's Street, except one house. Ceri's. The bell under my finger rang hollow and echoing. From an upstairs window in the next house a woman I couldn't see called out, 'Not at home. They had to go in the middle of the night. Mrs Price's sister Olwen took seriously ill in the port.' I thanked her and walked back up the street, cursing the fog, sulking again, a child left out of the game. I wasn't going to see what they were playing at out there on Garston's farm. To hell with it. And once more that bloody poem in my head.

'Goodness,' Miss Phelps said. 'Philip Roberts. One has to be careful who one opens one's doors to.' Another inch of door space, another part-face. 'Philip Roberts? Are you the one who received a decoration for gallantry?'

'That's Emlyn Morton.' And the door was opened wide. I nearly laughed aloud, having forgotten what a little round dumpling of a woman she was. Miss Dorothy Phelps, English Lit.

'You were in the fifth when I retired. You joined the Navy?'

'The army.' She led me into her sitting room which had a second fog from cigarette smoke.

'And it was North Africa?'

'Burma.' She had five wireless sets, a notebook by each one.

'Father a butcher?'

'Bookseller.'

She did a little dance and clapped her hands. 'Ah. Yes. Got it! Emlyn Morton's crowd.' Her voice which had boomed Shakespeare, Tennyson and Keats was ragged. 'I have been trying to forget you all. A poem you say?' She accepted a cigarette eagerly. 'Your interest in poetry then was minimal, surely? Sit. Cup of tea?' By Laura's standards the room was dirty. Miss Phelps moved a vacuum cleaner and went through into the kitchen to put the kettle on the stove. 'Forty years I spoke,' she went on, 'now I listen to my wireless. Philip Roberts, Philip Roberts – so many Robertses and Joneses and Williamses. Radio Paris in ten minutes! And you want the school magazines? Astonishing.'

She went on hunting in sideboards and cupboards, treated me to a bottoms up view of a pair of blue bloomers and brown stockings, and refused all offers of help, muttering my name as she did so. She came back with a large, cardboard box, paused to light yet another cigarette before she opened it. 'Did you say 1937?' Yellowing, typewritten sheets in her hands, but there was no poem by Edward Mortimer in that issue.

'Will you try 1938?'

She held up a stubby finger for silence, the cigarette smoke bringing tears. 'Edward Mortimer. Philip, we never had an Edward Mortimer. I would have remembered that one. But we – ah, yes – we had a little joke. She smoothed down a page. 'Yes, yes. We had a joke.' She cleared her throat and croaked it out:

Who's left to love?
Only he who rages –
Gone to ashes all the ages.
Summer has a fine warm face,
Winter such a cold embrace.'

And we were silent. The time for Radio Paris was long since past. She gave me a long, questioning look. 'By Edward Mortimer. Did you know that not one member of staff, none of the children, not one parent ever asked me who Edward Mortimer was! And what does that prove? Why – that nobody ever reads school magazines.'

'Emlyn?' I said.

She nodded. 'He and Marshall Edmunds came to see me – here, in this house. Mrs Edmunds, I was told – is it true?'

'Yes.'

Another cigarette appeared in her mouth.

'Incredible. It is many years since I saw her. I don't get out much, you see. Never a mixer.' She traced the words with a nicotine stained finger. 'Children come up with a promising idea, you know – in poetry I mean. They look as if they are going to take you somewhere

– then they quit. This is what has happened here. The first three lines promise something, however obscure, and then we go onto something else entirely. It has little meaning out of context. Such a private poem, wouldn't you say? I said to him "you never wrote this, Morton" but he was a beautiful boy, you know, a charmer. Claimed Edward Mortimer was his nom de plume. I never knew if he had penned it or not. But in it went. A bit of a joke.' Ash from her cigarette fell on the paper and she blew it away. 'A private poem. It can mean anything you want it to. Like a prayer.'

She shivered visibly. She stared, a plump and solemn owl, questions gathering behind the cigarette smoke. 'Why do you want to know? As a young man you did not exhibit either a great concern or feeling for poetry – although I may of course have misjudged you – now home from the war...'

'I don't know. It was just something that was going through my head. Look – thank you very much, Miss Phelps. I'll be going. Sorry to put you to any trouble.'

I got to my feet and she followed me down the hallway to the door, but at a distance. I opened the door, and then she spoke, 'His mother had died that winter. I saw it as an obscure elegy for her. Gossip said his father was having an affair at the time. Such a private poem.'

How tiny she was in the gloom of the hall, running a hand through her short grey hair. I apologised again and stepped out into the fog. She came in a rush to push the door to. 'It's very important, isn't it?' She called after me, a kind of relief in her voice.

'No, not really,' I replied, but it was important. I felt as if I was nearly there. I walked home slowly, and each face in the fog was Idwal Morton's.

Laura was in the kitchen, pouring herself a glass of stout. 'What have we here,' I said. 'I thought you'd signed the pledge.'

She kept her face hidden. 'No jokes required,' she said and gulped down half a glassful. 'The wedding will not now take place! He's changed his mind.'

'Well – good God – what came over him? I'll go and sort him out for you.'

She became suddenly vicious. 'Don't you think you've done enough? All of you? All these terrible things that have happened?' Laura in tears. 'Like he said – as a man in business in the town he can't afford to have his name mixed up...'

'Can't afford what? Does he think I've been murdering people?'

'You've been involved – and people talk...'

'The miserable old sod!' How many wrong things can you say? 'If you ask me – you're well rid of the bloody old skinflint!'

Then she looked up, her face stiff as a mask, her voice filmed with ice. 'Did it never strike you that I liked him?' I had to look away, and the silence grew around us. I wanted to say I was sorry, but it was too late for that. J. Palmer Roberts' son – your father always laughed at me.

I was still wearing my raincoat. 'I have to go out, Laura,' I said. 'I'm sorry.' But she made no reply.

XV

The fog had taken over space and time. No distance and limited sphere of vision, no longer a meaning to day or night. I stamped angrily through it, sometimes misjudging the corner of a building, bumping against a lamp post, colliding with a pillar box that should not have been there. Heading for nowhere and with no purpose. The ships cried out to one another in the estuary, a new urgency in their sound, a new poignancy too. And the fog was colder now and in its mass a smell of burning. It had to be opening time somewhere, please God.

I was the first customer of the evening in the King's Arms. The barman, Matthew Hughes, said the old man and Emlyn had not put in an appearance during the afternoon opening, and hadn't things gone chronic what with these women getting knocked off and this bloody fog putting the kibosh on everything? 'Mrs MT, man – Christ!' His brother had taken six hours to cover two miles of his bread round in the old van. Out in the country, see. 'Know that old Tower on the old coast road there? My brother seen a battalion of police out there, man. Diggin' inside the bloody thing. Tell me what for?' Matt's questions were usually rhetorical, but this time he waited, eyebrows pointing, for an answer.

'Ghosts, Matt,' I replied, and downed my drink and headed for the door. I wanted company, but I wanted to keep on the move, too – and a little of Matt went a long way at the best of times.

Amos would be back by now, surely? I called in at the Royal on the off chance, and killed conversation dead. No old man perched on a stool there, either. I could put a name to every face around the bar, but every face belonged to a stranger, suspicious and calculating and sly.

When they started talking again they were talking for my benefit, inviting comments. George Garston's lad gone funny while studying over there in London. Police put out a general warrant, so they had. 'I've heard it's all got to do with some photographs taken some time ago,' someone said. It was then that I began to fear for Amos Ellyott's safety.

Mrs Edmunds had entered Amos's rooms in search of more examples of the art of a Polish Airman. The killer too. I shivered. And the killer would have worked it out that Amos Ellyott had not surrendered everything to the police. The old goat had never in his life made a present of secrets. He thrived on secrecy; had it on toast at every meal. The great detective: he'd played that role all around the town. Mrs Edmunds had been in possession of photographs, and had been silenced. And that made Amos the next on the list.

I didn't really care much whether or not Amos lived or died. But fearing for him, at that time was at least something positive, something to act on.

'Oh – you is it, Philip?' Miss Williams said. 'Strangers ringing my bell all day. Don't you think everything's gone strange?'

'Is he back, Miss Williams?'

'Who? Mr Rude? That's what I call him. Oh, yes – he came back – smelling of manure and soaking wet. Mr Rude and Smelly.' She tittered nervously and touched her mouth. 'He's not going to stay in my house much longer I can tell you.'

'Well – may I see him? Was Emlyn Morton with him?'

'Both of them stinking,' she said. 'Messed up my bathroom. Left smells everywhere – and out they went again. He called Emlyn Morton his bodyguard!'

'Did he say where they were going?' Her narrow head shook a negative. 'Did he leave a message, then?'

'For you, Philip? Your name was never mentioned in my hearing.' Great, I thought, great. 'Besides,' she added in a voice laced with spite, 'you're not supposed to ask great detectives where they're going, are you? That's what I told George Garston's boy.'

'Davy Garston? Has he been here?'

'No more than an hour ago. He had his coat up – like this.' She cupped her face in her hands. 'Wanted to speak to Mr Ellyott. He looked very strange. You all look very strange. I don't know what the world is coming to...'

'Miss Williams – if Davy Garston comes back don't let him in, all right? On no account.'

She drew herself up to her full height, which wasn't much. 'Don't you worry,' she said. 'Nobody comes in this house. I've told the Police about David Garston.'

Davy Garston fits. I was trying to persuade myself as I climbed the stairs to Amos's rooms. I was in time to catch Mr Stubbs as he came out and turned the key in the door. Stubbs didn't like me. He didn't look as if he liked anyone very much.

'Of course he isn't in. Been ordered to stop out, hasn't he?'

'You've not seen him?'

Mr Stubbs shook his polished head. 'Not today, thank God. I've told them it's a case of red herrings. They shouldn't keep listening to old cranks.'

'The Tower, you mean?'

He gave me a superior smile. 'The Tower if you like. Everything if you like.' He stepped past me on to the stairs. 'There's been interference,' he added heavily. 'You know about that – the interference that's gone on. You seen anything of Davy Garston?'

'What d'you want Davy Garston for?'

He took a couple of aggressive steps back up. 'You trying to be funny, mister?'

'I don't have to try – comes naturally.' Davy Garston, I thought, and why not? He was a match fit.

'Listen, Sonny Jim – you are not in the clear by any manner of means.' Mr Stubbs was wearing his mean and nasty look.

I walked straight for him, and around him down the stairs and into the fog, into no man's land.

David Garston the match fit. He'd had a breakdown in London. He was hitting the bottle. He was one of Lilian's callers. He had medical knowledge and would know all about pressure points in the neck. A dead cert, old Davy. I went marching through the fog to the Crescent in order to give them the benefit of my reasoning. Davy Garston had links through his father with murky goings on in the past. There was a light on downstairs. I walked up the steps of the porch. Davy Garston would have access to a key for the Market

Hall. Everything going for Davy. I raised a hand to knock on the porch door. Above all, Davy Garston had done a bunk and was on the run with a general warrant chasing after him... Oh, balls. I backed out of Idwal's porch and headed for the pub circuit in search of the great detective and his bodyguard.

It was a thin night for the brewers. The fog had sealed off the town, nailed the customers behind their own front doors – unless there was something good on the wireless, but that was hardly likely. Only the hard-core were out, blue veins in their noses, blood in their eyes, hands that had only recently stopped shaking, cigarettes going like Roman candles. And they were hostile, too, all staring and corner mouthed whispers and now and then a loud challenge across the room. 'Reckon us boys ought to turn up for this Town Meeting they've called – eight o'clock tonight – all us interested parties. In the Town Hall.' The mean old heart of the town, the lynch mob who would never leave a drink on the counter to do anything, anytime. And everywhere I drew a blank. No master criminologist and his assistant sighted anywhere. They were probably nose down, like blood hounds in the fog, following clues.

I tried Ceri's house again, still without lights, no one at home, not even a comment from the old bird next door. I went tramping again, something burning now on the go, the long braying of the sirens, mocking me. Perhaps I ought to stay in one place for Amos to find me. But I couldn't stop. I went up and down Liverpool Street twice before I called in the house. Laura was sitting in the kitchen still, a new bottle of stout on the table. She indicated the envelope that had come for me, pushed through the letter box, and no sign of the sender in the street. The note was brief: 'THE MARKET HALL AT 7. URGENT'. It was signed Andrei Ridetski.

The padlock in the gates of the Market Hall would not take my key. I examined it. A new padlock. Another message. I walked around the building to the garage at the back, and there again the police guard had been dropped. Everybody out with a pick and a shovel, everybody hunting Davy Garston in the fog.

I pulled at the central door of the garage. It opened. I stepped inside. The door was swinging shut behind me. And there was someone there. I could sense it. The hairs at the back of my neck responded to it. Black in there. Smell of oil. I thumbed the wheel on my lighter. It fired first time. Someone there all right. He had a twelve bore pointing straight at me. As much as I could see before my lighter went out. Black as the coal house now. George Garston's voice, high pitched, stretched tight, quavering, 'Stick your hands up, Andy!'

The electric light bulb above my head exploded into life. For something less than a blinding second I thought the twelve bore had gone off. 'Why, Philip, goodness me, is it you?' He sang it, standing there one foot in front of the other, pointing the gun at me. I was standing close to the back door of a huge old black car, straight out of the gangster flicks, caked with dust and hung with cobwebs. There were bits of old engines on the floor, God knows how many tyres, some milk churns and pieces of broken furniture. Behind Garston was the wall of the Market Hall, a narrow open doorway in it with a thick rope inside that made me think of the gallows. George Garston looked as if he was stuck there. 'Philip,' he said, 'did Andy send for you, too?'

'Andy who?'

'You know.' George was about done, his narrow face the colour and texture of lard, thick black stubble like a rash, black shadows under his eyes. 'Andy Ridetski – have you seen him?'

'I thought they were having a dig for him.' I motioned for him to lower the gun, but the man was stuck and the twin barrels, unfortunately, were stuck on me.

'Digging for Ridetski,' he said, contempt in his voice. 'He was a clever man, Andy. He could run rings around anybody.'

'Yet you thought I was Andy.'

'I never said that. Never. It was dark. I couldn't see who it was.' A silence fell between us. Then I suggested that it must be a strain holding a heavy gun like that, but he never moved and the black eyes of the gun stared fixedly at an area somewhere below my rib cage. I toyed with the idea of moving, to the left or to the right, just to see what he'd do. Only toyed with it, though.

'We aren't making any progress,' I said. 'What about some facts? Number one – Mr Ridetski is sending out invites. Number two – your David is wanted by the police.'

The gun dipped alarmingly, and I thought what have I done.

'That is all nonsense, I tell you. David is completely innocent. I have proof. It's Mr Ellyott – he's plotting against me. Plotting everything.' His eyes flashed wild and white. 'He's been digging in my yard! He's been leaving buttons on my doorstep!'

'Buttons? What kind of buttons?'

'From the RAF uniform! What do I want with

buttons? What do I know about buttons?' The gun swung up then down to support the appeal in his voice. 'RAF buttons on my doorstep! There are no RAF buttons in my yard. Philip – is Mr Ellyott insane?'

'Almost certainly,' I said.

'Saying lies about David. Saying lies about me. Saying lies about David and getting him nearly arrested. I never tried to shoot him. It was David!'

'David tried to shoot Mr Ellyott? What about me? I was there as well.'

'I never said that. No, no, no!' The blank and threatening eyes of the gun looked all around the garage. 'David was shooting those old crows. He didn't know Mr Ellyott or anybody was there. It's his nerves, you see. The examinations for a doctor are very difficult.' He gave out a long, shuddering sigh. 'If they can't find him then it's the fault of the police – because he isn't running away, because he's innocent!' The prominent Adam's apple in his scrawny neck rose and dipped but the gun remained steady, pointing.

'Maybe your family shouldn't play with guns,' I suggested.

He didn't appear to hear me. 'I couldn't say anything because they would have said things about David because his nerves are bad. People like a chance to be spiteful. But there was no intent you see. All those police digging inside that old Tower. That old thing. They wouldn't listen to me. It was in a very bad state and I set to at once, to mend it. Oh, some years ago now. I put some concrete inside it, you know – to hold it – and I tried to do a bit of pointing. But it isn't well built at all – not a proper tower or anything like that. It's the truth, Philip. You've got to tell Mr Ellyott. I'm just a poor working farmer. He's playing games with me. My son is completely innocent. I am completely innocent. It's David havin' trouble with his nerves – after the exams. You've got to explain to Mr Ellyott. You're his right-hand man.'

'Tell him yourself. He's probably waiting up there.'

'I was going to tell Andy to tell him. He was a good friend of mine, Andy...'

'Is that why he sent you those photos?'

'All false, them pictures. He'd made them up!'

'You got another one a few days ago – was that fake too?'

The twelve bore waved about but there wasn't much menace in it. 'All false them photos. He'd made them up. I took them to an expert and he showed me how Andy had done them up. For a joke, you see...'

'Which is why you stopped handing out the cash?'

His voice dropped to a grating whisper. 'You don't make a fool out of me, mister! Nobody makes a fool out of me.' An arrogant twist at his mouth.

'OK – Ridetski sent you the first lot of pictures?'

'I never said that. You're putting words in my mouth.'

'Sorry – but do you know who sent you the last one?'

He gave out a growl which I took to be a laugh. 'That Mr Ellyott of course.' He paused for some time, his mouth moving, eyes narrowing as he weighed up the way the conversation was going. 'It's all supposing, isn't it? If I got some old photo – which I'm not saying I did – it would be Mr Ellyott. Another of his tricks.'

'Not Mr Ellyott,' I said, hoping it was true.

For the first time the twelve bore pointed away from me. He cradled the gun in the crook of his left arm. 'You know who it was, Philip?'

'Certainly. It was Mrs Edmunds who sent you that photo.'

It nearly knocked him over. 'Never,' he snarled. 'Never, never, never. Sent it for that big talker MT, you mean? Oh, never, never, never! It was Mr Ellyott who told you to say that!'

And the gun went off.

A twelve bore going off is best appreciated if it is fired inside a corrugated iron garage. I thought the roof had blown out. Pellets whined around me, rebounding off the ancient car. And in the middle of it all there was the terrible crackle of broken glass. The car's windscreen had blown out.

I had gone down on my knees, arms up to protect my face. When I looked up it was the deathly quiet after thunder. George Garston was standing over me, and he was blubbering, broken. 'It was an accident, Philip. An accident, an accident.' He went blundering past me, making no effort to see if I was all right. And the sounds coming from him were of an animal in pain. He had a struggle with the door, then he charged out into the fog and the door slowly swung back into place.

The silence was deafening. I stood there and waited for the rush. Surely to God the entire neighbourhood must have heard the gun go off, but no one came running to the door, and inside the lift the rope hung stiff and still.

I had blood on my cheek, a trickle running down to the corner of my mouth. I wiped it away, more blood on my handkerchief than I had expected. I went over to the lift, broken glass grinding under my shoes. Only one way to go now, up a dark shaft to where there was a faint chink of light. I tried not to guess who would be up there. Not Ridetski, for sure. I climbed in. You sat with the rope running free between your legs. One way to go, and I admired myself for being so calm, blood on my face and all, until I began to pull on the rope. How easy it was, so little effort required to rise into the darkness, the wheels drumming above. Then everything closed in on me. How did you stop the bloody thing? But the time I drew level with the chink of light I was in a panic and pulling too fast. I yanked up on the rope and came to a lurching halt. And then I was scratching feverishly for the catch to the door, sweat breaking out on my forehead. My fingers found the catch. The door opened and I stumbled into the secret room. Two hurricane lamps on a table. Amos behind the table. A stranger in a white raincoat sitting at one end. Empty chairs in front of the table. Amos wore a hat with a wide brim. He had a black automatic in his hand, pointing at me. A night for cowboys, I thought. A night for a showdown.

XVI

'Ah,' Amos said, 'Philip Roberts. Come up to the light.' He placed the pistol carefully on some papers in front of him. 'You are the first to accept Mr Ridetski's invitation.'

The stranger was a big man with awkward movements, broad in the shoulder but not perhaps as broad as the raincoat suggested. A fancy dresser, he had a long lean face with dark, swarthy skin. Cheapened by a two piece moustache which made him look like a city con man. He had a gold tooth, a gold ring on his left hand. 'Pleased to meet you,' he said, smiling. 'Got a bad leg – excuse me.' He sounded more cockney than Polish.

'Mr Ridetski broke a leg some years ago,' Amos explained. 'It was set very badly.' He pushed back his hat. 'You have blood on your face. Did someone try to shoot you?' With a wave of his hand he indicated that I was to sit next to him, at the opposite end of the table from Ridetski. 'I take it you haven't seen Mr Ridetski before?' I shook my head. 'Philip,' he told the stranger, 'distrusts me because he is in awe of my mental powers – is that not so, Philip?'

'Just tell me what the hell you're doing up here.'

'Philip found the war tolerable only if he stopped

thinking.' He did his cackling laugh. 'Where were you all day? Emlyn was asking for you. Have you seen him?' Again I shook my head. 'There's blood on your face. We heard a noise which we took to be gunfire...'

'Garston's cracked up,' I said. 'He shot his car down there. You've overdone it. Scared the bugger off.'

The old man made irritable noises. 'This is a grave matter,' he responded sharply. 'We are here to conclude it. The end justifies the means.'

'That's a load of fucking bullshit, Amos. You want to be the main man, don't you? Playing God. That's why you picked this place and got your lanterns out and delivered your invitations and made sure nobody can come up here except by that bloody lift. That's why you've had the police running around in circles.' My voice echoed back at me from the outer darkness, hollow and mocking.

It brought on a silence that lingered. The stranger shuffled his feet and made silent appeals to Amos and let me have the benefit of some heavy staring.

'I see,' the old man said at last. 'You disapprove of my methods, but you may yet find that I am not some avenging angel. May I ask you to describe your encounter with Mr Garston?' He smiled. 'Please, Philip?'

I went through it with them, and Amos nodded and didn't make a single interruption. When I had finished he said, 'The police have not found his son?'

'I wouldn't know. He called at your lodgings, wanted to talk to you.'

'That sounds promising. You got the impression that George Garston thought you were Ridetski?'

'Yes.' I glanced at the stranger. 'But you've scared him off.'

'We shall see.' Amos picked up the pistol and held it out to me. 'Philip, I would regard it a favour if you would have charge of this weapon.'

'No chance,' I said.

'Please?' I shook my head firmly and stuck my hands deep into my pockets. 'But – it is possible that an attempt will be made on my life.'

'Not before bloody time. There's nobody I want to shoot, you understand. Except you, maybe.'

Amos did his ticking noises then slipped the gun into his pocket. He appealed to the stranger. 'You see what I have to put up with?' Ridetski nodded and looked hard at me across the table. And a silence fell over us. It was totally quiet except for old men's noises – groans and sighs and creaks – coming from Amos. In the distance I thought I could hear the sirens from the ships in the estuary. The stranger kept on turning the gold ring on his finger. It was twenty minutes past seven, assuming my watch was behaving itself.

Then we heard the lift go down. 'Ah,' Amos said, 'the invited.' We listened for it to rise again, and the wheels rolled and we looked towards the door. The lift halted. Fingers scratched on wood. The door opened. Emlyn's grinning face. 'Second floor? Any more for the basement?'

He came into the light. He was wearing a pair of cord trousers, a white polo neck sweater under his RAF jacket which he had dyed black. 'What's all this, are we going to have a séance, or something? Hullo, Philip. That old bugger's been dragging me round all day. Who's that?' He pointed at the stranger. 'Is it the original Mr Ridetski in person?' He went over to the stranger and crouched and stared. 'Where did you dig him up from, Amos?' he said as he straightened.

He came over to sit next to me. 'Philip, I've been wallowing in bullshit all day. Smell me.' The old man cackled softly. 'I had to have three baths when I got home.' He smiled broadly at each of us in turn. 'Good evening,' he said. 'Good evening. Good evening.' And very softly, out of the corner of his mouth, started to trumpet 'Night and Day'.

'Desist,' Amos hissed at him. 'That damn noise – he's been making it all day.'

'You should have asked Philip. Five o'clock this bloody morning, Philip! Can you imagine? Silly old bugger!' The lift began to move. 'Ah! What light from yonder window breaks, I wonder?'

'Please be quiet,' Amos said wearily, but Emlyn was sitting up straight and saying 'Hark! Harken! Who can this be?' The lift had reached the bottom. The stranger fingering his moustache. The lift began to rise, and even Emlyn was quiet until the door opened.

'Oh, my God,' he said, 'father's been at the wine cellar again!'

Idwal Morton had a foolish, lopsided, brilliantly white grin on his face, but he looked better, his great forehead glistening, his eyes bright. He closed the door behind him. The lift began to move again. 'MT's on his way,' he said. He waited there in the outer darkness. 'MT,' he said again as the lift came up. When the door opened he nearly fell over as he bent to help MT Edmunds into the room. 'Good old MT,' he kept saying, 'steady as she goes.'

They came into the light, Idwal holding on to MT's arm and punching him gently. 'Thank you for your message,' MT said. 'What a terrible fog. The worst in living memory. Did you know there's a ship on fire in the estuary?'

'Gentlemen,' Amos said, 'may I introduce an old acquaintance of yours – Mr Andrei Ridetski.' The stranger looked uncertain, watching Amos as if he expected a signal.

MT looked at the Pole blankly. 'A freighter on fire in the estuary,' he said. He was wearing a black bow tie. I could see his fists clenching. 'There must have been a collision in the fog you see. Worst fog in living memory.'

But Idwal Morton went over to the man and resting both hands on the table looked down at him and said, 'Will you look at the way this one's filled out, MT. By God, you bloody old crook, Andy!'

'Please sit,' Amos ordered.

'Certainly,' MT said. 'Of course.' He kept his head rigid and stared straight ahead.

Idwal took the chair next to him after giving him a questioning glance. And now that they were in the light and seated they slumped suddenly, MT somehow punctured, Idwal ravaged, and both of them exhausted.

'You old piss pot,' Emlyn said to Idwal. 'You should be in your bed.'

'I do not want any idiotic remarks from you two,' Amos said, a steely note in his voice. 'I may lose the thread. I want no distraction.' He had a tattered bundle of notes in front of him. Most of them on the backs of envelopes. 'May I say at the outset that I respect your decision to accept Mr Ridetski's invitations. There should be three of you, but perhaps the third may yet change his mind. Only truth is on trial here, our purpose to make an enquiry into it, nothing more. I am pleased that you were able to greet one another without bitterness, more especially since you two gentlemen had it in mind, some years ago, to kill Mr Ridetski.'

'The photos were fakes,' Idwal said, his eyes shining.

'But you did not know that then, Mr Morton. Unlike the third man.'

'Comes up behind me, silent like a cat,' Ridetski said suddenly. 'One push and I'm down that lift shaft with a busted leg.'

'If you don't mind, Mr Ridetski,' Amos broke in.

'All right, all right – but I crawl away. I get a lift on a convoy out of this damn town, thank God. Too damn dangerous.'

'Mr Ridetski, please. I am very grateful to you for coming forward – but I must ask you to wait until I ask you to speak.' The Pole raised both hands, palms outwards, and nodded. 'You did very well from your experiments in the dark room. A venture not without profit, although one gentleman soon refused to pay. What a greedy man you were, Ridetski. Three men...'

'The war wasn't going to go on forever, Mr Ellyott. War is a greedy business.'

A silence followed the Pole's remark. Amos looked as if he had already lost the thread and was shuffling his papers. Six of us around a table, the oil lamps flickering. Idwal and MT stared fixedly ahead, the Pole with an injured look on his face, Emlyn working away at yet another trumpet break which I could not identify. A stranger coming upon us might well think that we were a secret society, or bank robbers met to divide the loot. I kept my mind on fancies in order to keep reality away.

'To resume. Ridetski increased his demands. Two men decide on the short answer.' I could see sweat breaking out on Idwal's forehead. 'Ridetski is summoned to a meeting here, in this room. Here among the bags of sugar, the tinned meats, the jars of coffee, spirits in bottles, tobacco and cigarettes by the box. The currency of war. The currency still in the piping days of peace. Ridetski arrives early, to hand over negatives he might claim now, though I would doubt it.' The Pole raised his shoulders in a non-committal shrug. 'But let that pass. What matters here and now is that he was standing, crouched perhaps, over the door to that lift shaft, waiting and listening. And someone...'

'Garston it had to be,' Ridetski broke in.

'Someone.' Amos raised his voice. 'Someone kneed you in the back and sent you down the lift shaft. By some miracle, Mr Ridetski's injuries were limited to a broken leg. But he was trapped there at the bottom of the shaft. And on the way were two men.' Ridetski nodded sombrely. 'A predicament indeed. Was it fear that gave you the strength to drag yourself out to the inspection pit?'

MT stood and raised a hand.

'Sit down sir,' Amos ordered. 'There will be time for questions later.' MT nodded and resumed his seat. And I knew it all then.

'When the two gentlemen arrived there was no one here. Mr Ridetski crawled away, secured a lift out of the town...'

MT was on his feet again, 'With the court's permission I would like to point out...'

Once again Amos waved him down. 'When I have done,' he went on. 'Mr Ridetski left in chilling circumstances. He deserted. Began a new life, leaving behind him photographs and negatives, some of which poor Mrs Edmunds was to discover and remove when she paid a visit to a hairdresser's establishment on a fateful night.' Amos blew his nose into his handkerchief, a sound that made echoes in the room. 'Mrs Ridetski had left in a hurry, her door ajar, to keep a most fearful appointment...'

Now MT was up again, standing to attention. This time the words would not come out, and all he could manage was to raise both arms to Amos, a gesture of surrender.

'Tweedledum,' Emlyn said softly. 'What about Tweedledee?' But Idwal made no move to stand. He was looking up in wonder at MT and with shaking hands tugged at his coat. MT came down heavily on his chair, his mouth moving, no sound coming out. And there was a silence that seemed to last forever.

Then Amos cleared his throat. 'Not consistent with the facts, Mr Edmunds? No one left the town nursing a broken leg? No one pushed down a lift shaft on that night in October 1942?' MT staring ahead again. 'My apologies for the charade. I was at a loss, I must confess. Someone concealed a body that night. Mr Garston, Philip tells me, expected to see Ridetski tonight. I accept that. You, Mr Morton, imagined a likeness in our friend here.' He looked at the stranger at the head of the table. 'But you, Mr MT, knew quite well it could not possibly be Ridetksi, did you not?' MT rose once more, Idwal staring at him aghast. Amos motioned him down with a gentle wave of his hand. 'You, Mr MT alone.' Why didn't you just ask the man, I wanted to say? Why did he have to piss about like this? But he wasn't done yet.

He pulled something out of his pocket and tossed it on the table. I hated him then. It was a brass button. It did a spin on the scarred table top. It came to rest.

The silence stretched on. The whole room surely could hear the hammering of my heart. Then the man who had played Ridetski said, 'Where do we go from here, Mr Ellyott?' And at that moment the lift began to move and we sat in a burning silence waiting for it to rise.

It was David Garston who came out of the lift. David Garston, so pissed he fell out of the lift. 'I've come to confess,' he said, 'actually.'

David's legs were made of jelly. He took a couple of wobbly steps and decided that there wasn't much point in doing that. He had a smile on his face which did not belong there, and which he found an annoyance, and could do nothing about. He stared at us through a curtain of hair, blinked rapidly and tried again, fighting to keep us in focus. We were too much for him. His head sagged. His knees gave way. He crumpled slowly and came down heavily on his bum and found the wall against his back a comfort. His feet came up briefly, came down again with a thump. And he was gone. Out for the count.

'Oh, very well done,' Emlyn remarked. He went over to him and examined him with interest. 'What a lovely condition,' he said. 'What with shortages I didn't think there was that much booze left in town. What, do you suppose he came to confess to?' He lit a cigarette and had a spell of coughing and stubbed it out angrily. David Garston began to snore.

'A good case could be made for him. He was a caller

at the hairdresser's establishment. He did not sit out the concert with his parent on the night in question. He would have access to the keys which afforded an entrance to this wretched place. And he had suffered a breakdown, I understand. Much going for him. He would know the lady's history, have an inkling perhaps of involvement by his father in past misdemeanours. He would know that by making a telephone call in Ridetski's voice, he would bring her here. And he could have been waiting in the darkness for her, naked.'

'Oh, I say,' Emlyn said softly.

'And his motive? Threats to inform his father by that unfortunate lady? He might equally have been motivated by a desire to protect his father. Filial loyalty, perhaps? But this I would doubt. David's relationships with his parent were not good. He does not want to be a doctor. He has suffered a nervous collapse...'

'Especially now, eh Philip,' Emlyn said. The two broken men sitting in front of Amos were not listening, I was certain.

'His mind may, as they say, have snapped – and that would neatly account for later outrages. Oh, yes, he fits many parts of our puzzle. Who knows what he intended? But we do know, don't we, that the murderer returned to this place and carried Mrs Ridetski's body to the roof and hurled her into the night. The medical student might well know about pressure points in the neck, but physically he would be incapable, surely, of carrying an inert body up there for the final, perplexing act?' And he turned to me. 'Would you like to say something at this stage, Philip?'

'What would you like me to say, Mr Ellyott?' There was a tightening band across my stomach, a pulse beat jarring in my throat.

'You know, don't you?' An ancient face that should have emerged from under a protective shell. 'You have known for some time, I suspect. I would like you to say Emlyn, Philip.'

The silence choked me. Idwal Morton gave me one, pleading glance, and then his head went down.

'Say Emlyn, Philip boy,' Emlyn said softly.

'Emlyn who pilfered the key from Garston. Emlyn who telephoned the lady, a voice out of Middle Europe saying "This is Andy". Emlyn who waited her arrival in this room. Emlyn who returned later with Marshall Edmunds and told him to carry her up those stairs and throw her over the side.'

Two beaten men, heads lowered as if in prayer. The sound of their heavy breathing. David Garston snoring at the edge of darkness. My heart's pounding adding to the sound.

'Say Emlyn, Philip,' Emlyn said.

'A special relationship,' Amos said. 'Philip he admired. Marshall he controlled.'

'We're back to charades, Philip,' Emlyn's voice nagging at me. 'Join in. Say Emlyn.'

'Mrs Ridetski had become a rival,' the old croaking voice went on. 'Marshall became murderous, thinking it was Emlyn he saw leaving the lady's house, mistaking David Garston for him.'

David Garston gave out a light, yelping snore.

'Well – you've got to admit it's an interesting proposition,' Emlyn said, 'considering I was blowing my lungs out at that dance at the Royal, with witnesses to prove it.'

'Such a drunken affair,' Amos remarked coldly.

'With long intervals to use up the special license at the bar. He was away only a short time. She came hurrying through the streets. He stripped off and waited for the lift to rise...'

'Oh, come on!' Emlyn said. 'Then back to the dance in his birthday suit?'

'And Marshall, to seal their special relationship, had to cast her away from him forever.' The old man's voice cockerel high. The terrible acceptance from the two men. 'The total irrationality of it. Inviting attention to this wretched but special place.'

'Now look, Philip, you'd better say Emlyn because this old bugger's getting a bit rude.'

'Next day,' Amos went on, 'he was to realise what a natural suspect Marshall Edmunds made. Especially when he confessed. And so it had to become a dreadful farce. A mass-murderer has to arrive on the scene.' An old man's mockery in his voice. 'Ghastly charades. Tiny, fragile women. Miss Porterhouse on the King's lap, Miss Sweeney among the flowers, Mrs Palmerstone cast adrift. Essays in the grotesque. We were to think, of course, that there was a frenzied killer at large, but in truth one suspects, were it possible, something even more sinister. Self gratification, dare I suggest?'

'You suggest anything you like,' Emlyn said lightly, 'but you're a bit short of proof.'

Speak up, I wanted to cry out to the two bowed heads across the table. For Christ's sake. Just one word of protest. Someone please.

'And finally, Mrs Edmunds.' MT shook his head, forcing himself not too look up. 'Mrs Edmunds who linked old misdemeanours with new outrages. Fearing for her son she circulated photographs...'

'It was for the boy!' MT gasped out.

'One of them she brought to me. Why to me? Emlyn wondered what I had done to make her show her hand. I informed him that I had more photographs. He never asked me where I had obtained them, but he was not long in making the connection with a length of wallpaper removed from Mrs Ridetski's rooms.' He stuck a cigarette in his mouth and moved it about arrogantly but made no effort to light it. 'Thus he came plundering to my rooms. He knew I was close. He had to find how close. And tragically Mrs Edmunds arrived at the same conclusion. Unlike Mr Garston I have no faith in locks and keys.'

'Except that he was at the pictures with Ceri Price,' I said.

'Philip!' Emlyn's voice ringing in my ears. 'Good old Philip! One flaw destroys it all. All these lovely theories blown to smithereens. Got you now, Sherlock!'

And still two men with heads bowed, locked in silence. Amos Ellyott stroked his nicotine stained moustache, then pulled a gold watch from the depths of his clothing and snapped it open. He gave a nod. 'I gave you time, all of you. Emlyn, you didn't have to come here this evening...'

'Good story, Amos. I wouldn't have missed it for the world.'

A long drawn-out sigh from the old man. 'You could have gone anywhere but you went immediately to an address I gave you.' He waved a hand at the man who had played Ridetski. 'This gentleman's niece and her husband have taken a boarding house in the town. It was there that I told you I had moved the young lady and her family. A lie – as you discovered.

They are elsewhere in town.' He turned to me. 'Emlyn left the cinema at half past eight and did not return. Miss Price, a most loyal young lady, was a long time admitting the fact. I ordered her to wait until eight this evening, then she was to inform the idiot Inspector. I needed time for men to think and make decisions.'

David Garston snored in the silence, then Emlyn laughed.

'I am nearly done,' Amos said. 'And what is left?' He glanced at the man who had played Ridetski. 'The first death. The unknown death. Andrei Ridetski.' A gasping sigh from Idwal Morton. 'Polish Airman, petty thief, photographer, greedy blackmailer – a death from which all else follows.'

I saw MT nod his head decisively. The sweat was beaded on Idwal's dome.

'In October 1942, the depths of the war,' Amos resumed, once again addressing himself to me, 'Emlyn came home for a weekend's leave. Marshall Edmunds was on his way to the Middle East. Emlyn returned to find his father richer than of late, but a victim now of an extortioner who had to be eliminated.' Amos brought his fist down on the table. The lanterns shuddered. 'Good God, did you all think the damn war was going to go on forever? We must assume that Emlyn overheard snatches of conversation between his father and MT. He was convinced that they would botch it – as they had botched most things in their lives. So he intervened. Here in this foul place then cluttered with illicit merchandise. Twenty four hours later he was on a raid into Germany.'

'Strike the gong,' Emlyn murmured.

'As you heard tonight, it was Mr MT Edmunds

who discovered the body and cleaned up the mess.' Suddenly he swung his baleful stare from me to Emlyn. 'Here,' he said, tapping the back of his neck, 'there is a trigger point, is there not? The noose is purely to occupy the victim's hands?'

'If you say so, oh wise one,' Emlyn replied genially, 'but you're still very thin on proof.'

Amos puffed out his cheeks. 'Proved by silence here and now, wouldn't you say? Proved by a button or two?' He fumbled in his pockets and tossed two buttons in the air. They fell together on the table. One of them spun off on to the floor. No one went after it. 'Tap the wall in the lift shaft as you ascend. Examine the panelling on the cavity wall. You will find loose boarding. Thrust your hand through and you will discover, among other items, more buttons. Where MT concealed the body. From the beginning you see, there was only one question – where is Ridetski?'

MT looked up. His face was blotched and tear stained. The lift was on the move again. David Garston snored. 'Can this be Garston senior, at last?' Amos enquired as it came up.

But it was Marshall Trevor Edmunds who struggled through the narrow doorway into the room.

XVII

'Shit!' Emlyn said with a laugh. He went over to the lift and there were whispers between them. Mash with his hand on Emlyn's shoulder. Emlyn clutching at Mash's sweater. Then Emlyn led Mash into the light, as if guiding a blind man. 'Come and join the party,' he said, 'although you've missed some very good stories.' They stood side by side, Mash towering above Emlyn; the boys caught in the act and all set to bluff it out. Emlyn elbowed Mash and Mash grinned slackly. 'It is suggested that we've buggered the job up,' he said.

I was nine. In the backyard of number 21 Liverpool Street, high stone walls on two sides, the green door taking up most of the third wall. A sun trap, and it was a hot day, heat coming up at me from the rough blocks of slate that covered the floor of the yard. There was a narrow flower bed where my mother had planted a climbing rose, tiny red blooms that now covered one wall. I was working on a raft – attempting to lash two empty oil drums to planks of wood found on the shore, and not having much success, on my knees there, sweating, the air heavy with the smell of roses. Then the green door was kicked open and Mash came into the yard, the snakes writhing in his hands. 'This one's bit me twice!' he said. Bramble scratches on his bare legs.

And there was a great, roaring shout as my father came bounding out of the house. Then the snakes were on the hot, grey slates, and my father's heel, steel protector flashing, came down on one tiny, darting head, then on the other. Blood on the slates. My father swearing as he bundled Mash into the house. Broken serpents, tails thrashing, at which I stared horror-struck. Then Emlyn appeared in the doorway, grey shorts and a blue shirt, and smiling of course, smiling. 'Well – what d'you think of that, Philip?' Spotless grey shorts, neat blue shirt, and smiling, smiling... Pick them snakes up, Mash boy. Go on – pick 'em up. The picture complete.

'The case is proved,' the old man said.

Mash wasn't looking at anybody, his lips moving soundlessly.

'You'll know everybody won't you Mash?' Emlyn doing the introductions. 'Our fathers. Old Philip. Say hello to Philip.' Mash's lips moving as if he was saying something to himself. 'And that was Mr Amos Ellyott who spoke just then.' Say hello to him as well.' Emlyn gave Amos a quick, stiff bow. 'And that's Davy Garston having a kip. And that's Mr Mystery, a wide boy if ever I saw one.'

'Donald Thompson,' the stranger said. He brought one hand on to the table. It held a flat, black automatic.

'Mash!' One word of command from Emlyn and Mash lunged forward and there was a great shout from Thompson as his chair tipped over backwards. The lamp at the end of the table was rocking. Mash had the gun in his hand.

'Drop it in my pocket,' Emlyn said. Thompson, out of breath, scrambled back on to his chair. 'My God, all this excitement's got my sinuses going.' Emlyn tapped his pocket. 'Good boy, Mash. Mr Donald Thompson doesn't look like a policeman to me, Mr Ellyott. Though they take all sorts nowadays, don't they?'

'Nobody took a gun off me before,' Thompson gasped. 'Not from the front...'

Emlyn sniffed. 'Destroys your sinuses the smell of gun oil. Mind you, Mash, old Philip may also have been issued with firearms – but old Philip isn't the type to flash it around, is he?'

'Emlyn!' A groan of despair from Idwal Morton.

'Sorry, father.' And Mash standing there, a protector ready to obey. Oh Christ, it was a world of strangers. Mash's lips moving. A poem to say like a prayer. A private poem that could mean different things to different people. My tongue was stiff and dry in my mouth.

'Emlyn – in the name of God!' Idwal Morton's face filmed with sweat. He was clutching at the edge of the table, the bone of knuckle white and shining.

'We're upsetting people, Mash. Time to dive out.' Emlyn smiled at Amos. 'The story finished? I take it you haven't got powers of arrest?'

'There is nowhere for you to go, Emlyn.'

'The Inspector on the right track at last? Haven't you led that man a dance! And him such an incompetent old fart, too! Close, is he? The cavalry on its way?'

'Nowhere for you to go,' Amos said again.

'Me and my big pal here? Nowhere to go? Nobody's got anywhere to go – that's the point, old boy!' He grinned at me and drew closer, standing behind Idwal. 'Whole fucking thing got out of hand, my old friend eh? Anyway – did I tell you I've got an audition with that band, Philip?'

I didn't answer him. Couldn't answer him.

Emlyn with a hurt expression on his face. Oh, God. I forced myself to look away. 'To the stairs, Mash boy,' he said. 'Get away time. Must be years since we climbed down from here in the dark.' That old, rust-bitten fire escape. Mash shambled over to the stairs. 'Time to say goodbye to the boys, Philip.'

Little Emlyn. He'd always had the ability to make you feel you had betrayed him. Even now.

'Ah, well. With apologies all round.' He touched Idwal's shoulder, and Idwal winced. He went running to the foot of the stairs and two of them, pushing each other and laughing, went scrambling up. We heard the door slam shut. Then MT was on his feet, bawling out a long, anguished protest, and Idwal Morton slumped forward on the table.

Inspector Marks came up the lift. It was a long time before he had sufficient men to batter down the door at the head of the stairs. 'Nobody up here,' someone called down. 'No signs sir.' The policemen came out of the lift, all of them strangers. Everywhere strangers. I helped to lift Idwal Morton on to a stretcher. An ebb and flow of men in the room. Lanterns everywhere. George Garston had made it at last. He was kneeling at David's side.

'We had to betray them by silence,' MT said. He was still sitting at the table. 'We realised it was what you intended for us to do, Mr Ellyott.' He should have spat in the old man's face, I thought. 'We never planned to kill anybody. Emlyn got it wrong.'

Inspector Marks had islands of red in his face and he was all belligerence. 'I'll have you know this man,' he cried, finger stabbing at Amos, 'is an imposter! He is not the great criminologist! Oh, no – he is only a distant cousin of the man!' He choked on the words. 'He is a writer of fiction, nothing more – for the blood and gore magazines, and story books for boys!'

No one took any notice of him, least of all Amos Ellyott. 'My last problem was who found Ridetski; who concealed his body,' he said to MT. 'And it was you alone, and you kept the secret.'

MT Edmunds stood to attention. 'It was my duty,' he said in a ringing voice. 'They were fighting for their country.' MT by name but not by nature. He shook hands first with me, then with Amos's bodyguard, then with the old man. He had always been a great hand shaker, and now he looked around wondering if he had missed anyone out, but nobody else seemed to want to take him on. With Stubbs at his side he marched out of the room to the top floor of the Market Hall, now lantern lit, arms swinging.

'You are an impostor, Mr Ellyott!' Inspector Marks resumed his attack. 'We have lost them because of your bloody interference!'

'Try not to be an idiot all the time, Marks,' Amos said. 'It was beyond your reasoning. My case from the start.'

Marks pawed at his face, shaking with anger. 'You held an unauthorised tribunal. An offence...'

'Say nothing, dear fellow,' Amos replied blandly. 'Say nothing. You'll be a Superintendent in six months.'

The Inspector went pounding to the stairs. Not for any special purpose, I felt – simply to get away from Amos. Thompson looked admiringly at Amos, 'I used to drive for Mr Ellyott you know, marvellous man.'

The policemen milled past us, most of them going up on to the roof. Amos gave out a long, shuddering sigh.

'What can they hope to find there? Oh, God, I am past weariness. Such an amusing boy – but flawed, I fear.' He lit a cigarette and shocked me by offering me one. 'I had to move the young lady and her family from their home, you know. Under great protest, naturally. But there was no other way. Emlyn called there not long after they had gone. And of course I had to keep him away from you.' He sighed again. 'You know, he was most co-operative, most concerned for my welfare – Philip – you knew, didn't you? You'd worked it out. Was it too unthinkable?'

George Garston went past the table, propping up David, who had a scarecrow grin on his face. 'I will say good night to you, then,' he said. 'What a terrible business, isn't it?' Amos ignored him.

'Poor Mrs Edmunds. Such false assumptions. Seeing a wheelbarrow, spades and cement at the Tower, she drew a false conclusion.'

Inspector Marks came stamping back. 'Do you intend to stay the night?' he roared at us. 'I want you all in the station. Now!'

Amos talked all the way along the top floor of the Market Hall, down the stairs. 'George Garston – the lesson in survival. Do nothing. Leave well alone.'

Outside my father's shop he gripped my arm. I shrugged him off. 'I was about to explain,' he said testily, 'that the young lady was a long, long time telling me what had caused him to leave the cinema so early. Yet another false assumption, Philip. You see – some chocolate she had in her handbag had melted, and as she offered a piece to Emlyn it fell in his lap – and she reached for it. And he was away instantly, obviously taking it to be a sexual advance! She was honest enough to admit that it could have been taken as such.' The fog was solid, packed tight at the gate of the Hall. 'He occupied Marshall. There is no other word for it.'

'Why don't you shut the fuck up?' I said and Thompson went *tut, tut.*

Amos carried on. 'And when Marshall had him by the throat he knew everything about himself.' Not then, I wanted to say. A hell of a long time before. A boy with vipers in his hands. But I couldn't tell anybody, least of all Amos Ellyott, something that had hidden itself in my memory.

We walked out into the fog. A smell of burning in the streets. The sirens in the estuary called to one another like beasts out of ancient time. 'Where would they head for, Philip?' The nagging old voice in my ear.

The fog would be especially thick on the dune. 'You know as well as I do,' I told him. There. To play at sailors.

Not until first light were they found. Emlyn was face down on the black mud. His neck was broken. Mash was asleep in the *Ariadne's* cabin. Summer's face now clouded and dark.

XVIII

When it was all over, everything said, judgements passed, I went down to the *Ariadne* on a late spring day with a can of paraffin and set light to her. With Mash away in a place that would, I hoped, have a rhythm to its day not unlike that of the army's, the boat was mine, and only fire seemed right for her. Ceri, also home for the weekend, joined me on the dune; stood silent at my side to watch. It was no go for us. Now we could only meet to mess about, kid each other, although I wanted it to be otherwise, guessed she might too.

A hesitant fire at first, but once it had hold the *Ariadne* blazed there on the mud, dissolved before our eyes in great tongues of flame, her timbers exploding. Out of the town the children came running – Robert Owen, Sian Thomas, Captain X among them – and they danced around her for a while, then crowded close to us, turning now and then to me as if an explanation were due for so loud, so violent a burning. Laura and Will Wilkins had also arrived, as had Amos Ellyott, but he stayed to one side, the man apart, sensing more ambiguities, I was certain, in this final, boyish act. I doubted if he would be thinking, as I was, of the day of MT's sports day, when the children were like skaters on that sodden track, and Emlyn and Mash out with the towels, and the shrieks, and the legs flying, and the laughter, and the searches in the long grass for the ones who had got lost.

Mari Stead Jones was eighteen when her father, the writer Stead Jones, passed away suddenly. She helped to pack up his papers into a large wooden chest, to be sealed until a time when the family could bear to look at them. In 2007, during the renovation of the family home, Mari discovered the chest tucked away in the back of a wardrobe – full of notebooks, unpublished manuscripts and plays.

Mari found herself drawn into the stories. She says, 'I picked up his notes for *Say Goodbye to the Boys*. And that was it; I was sold on the story. The characters and the plot made a great impression on me. I felt the language and the structure needed updating – it needed, in my humble opinion, work. I loved every minute of the labour – it was like being with someone again, who you have missed so terribly that your heart felt it would never recover and all of a sudden your heart feels full and sound and whole again. Truly cathartic.'

She began to tweak the notes here and there, first tentatively, then with enjoyment and growing confidence – exploring her own writing abilities in the process, something she feels Stead would have approved of greatly. It was words of encouragement from Phillip Pullman and Dai Smith at the launch of the Library of Wales edition of Make Room for the Jester in 2011 that persuaded her to publish *Say Goodbye to the Boys*.

Blackmail and murder make *Say Goodbye to the Boys* both a dark comedy and a quick-witted thriller. It's also surprisingly tender, a portrait of old friendships lived to the gentle rhythms of a sleepy, wave-lulled town in the warm face of summer. The novel proves that writing is a gift one can inherit, and introduces Mari as a comic writer of the first order.

Stead Jones, born Thomas Evan Jones in 1922, was brought up in Pwllheli, north Wales. His studies were halted by World War Two and five years in the British Army. After demobilisation he completed his degree and teaching qualifications and took the position of lecturer in Liberal Studies at Leyland Motors Technical College in Lancashire, where he remained until his retirement. His first novel *Make Room for the Jester* was published in 1964 in both the UK and the USA to much critical acclaim. Concerned that there might be a surfeit of Tom Jones's about – Tom Jones the movie, based on the book by Henry Fielding, was coming out, and a certain Welsh singer of the same name was gaining popularity – his agent at the time advised him to consider a pen-name. He took inspiration from his own father, nicknamed Stead Jones while manager at the Stead and Simpson shoe shop in the village. *The Ballad of Oliver Powell* followed in 1966, and then *The Lost Boy* in 1968. He carried on writing until he died in 1985.

"I was enchanted with it, not only for the memories of place and atmosphere it evoked so skillfully, not only for the light touch and the sympathetic voice of the narrator, but mainly for the brilliantly drawn portrait of an extraordinary individual."

Phillip Pullman, author of the *Northern Lights* trilogy

In Stead Jones's *Make Room for the Jester*, Lew Morgan and Gladstone Williams are two friends trying to make sense of their lives over a long hot summer. When the charming but drunk Ashton Vaughan returns home to Welsh seaside town Porthmawr – the "primeval swamp of respectability" – he triggers a chain reaction of ruin, disillusion and death which keeps the whole town bubbling for a summer that will change everything.

There's fraud, farce, drama, drunkenness, temperance, hysteria and tragedy in this 'Welsh *Catcher in the Rye*', a haunting journey from the edge of childhood into a threatening adult world.